A HEART REARRANGED

PEACOCK HILL ROMANCE BOOK 5

ELIZABETH MADDREY

For my Family

1

―――――

"**W**hy are you in here?"

Vanessa Fisher turned, scowling, and saw Topher Adams standing next to three large, rolling coolers with his hands on his hips. The guy might be hot, and his wedding cakes were amazing works of art, but he defined unfriendly and hard to work with. "Checking on the flowers. Which I see you moved. Again."

"They were in my way. I'll put them back when I'm finished setting up. I would think a professional florist like you would know better than to decorate the cake area before the cake is in place."

"Seems to me I got the same schedule you did. I just happened to stick to it."

Red flooded Topher's face and neck. His jaw twitched and he spoke through gritted teeth. "I kept Sean informed of the delay."

"Well he didn't say anything to me." Vanessa crossed her arms and held his stare. If he thought he was going to intimidate her, he had another think coming. The wedding planner should have kept her in the loop. She'd take that up with him later.

"And I believe Sean has talked to you about moving my flowers. Several times."

"They were in the way."

"They wouldn't have been if you'd been on time!" Vanessa took a deep breath and tried to focus over the blood thundering in her ears. She was not going to get into another shouting match with him. No matter how annoying and obnoxious he was.

"Whatever. I'll let you know when you can put stuff back. I'd planned to do it. It's not like it's hard."

She clamped her teeth together. She was not going to respond. Was. Not. Going. To. Huffing out a breath that was closer to a strangled scream, Vanessa spun on her heel and stomped from the climate-controlled tent into a wall of wet summer heat that exemplified Virginia in September.

The wedding planner jogged toward her, winding through the tables set up in front of the lion-head fountain, whose sprawling pool stretched the entire width of the area behind Peacock Hill. "Vanessa!"

She stopped and tapped her foot.

"Hey. Topher's a little behind schedule."

"I know that now." She glanced over her shoulder at the tent then frowned at Sean. "He moved my flowers."

Sean winced. "Sorry. I meant to let you know to shuffle the dessert tent to last. Did he say when he'd be finished setting things up?"

"Of course not. That would've been helpful. But after you find out, can you let me know?" She'd go double-check the flower setup in the foyer where the ceremony would take place. Maybe by the time she finished that, she could fix the flowers in the tent. She sure wasn't going to let Topher put things back.

Sean sighed and pinched the bridge of his nose. "Come on. Can't we all be adults?"

"I am not the one being childish here. That—he—argh!" She broke off as Sean strode into the tent. Fine. She followed him back into the cool tent. Let Topher explain his behavior with an audience. Of course, Topher and Sean were friends, so she'd probably still end up on the losing end.

"—that's why I called and said I was running behind. It's not my fault she put flowers in here before the cake was set. Seriously, who does that?"

"Someone trying to stick to the schedule she was given." Vanessa jumped in before Sean could speak.

Sean held up his hands. "Look, this is on me, okay? I get that. It's my bad. Vanessa, why don't you give Topher your cell number? Then he can text you when he's done in here and you don't have to wait for him to tell me and then for me to have time to let you know. Azure and the attendants are going to need their flowers soon. The foyer and staircase already look amazing, so I know you'll have time to get the tent finished before it becomes an issue."

"I can put everything back. I took pictures before I moved things." Topher waggled his cell phone. "It's not like it's hard."

"You will not touch the flowers again." Vanessa fought the urge to glare at Topher. She had to maintain some semblance of professionalism in front of Sean if she wanted him to keep sending business her way. She liked coming out to Peacock Hill. Sure, it was a bit of a hike from Richmond, but the venue was amazing. There were so many possible locations for a ceremony and reception. She'd been elated when Azure said the ceremony itself would be inside. Too bad the reception was out in the Labor Day swelter.

"Topher." Sean shot a firm glance toward the caterer. "He'll text you when he's set, right?"

"Fine." Topher held out his phone. "Put your number in. I'll label it later."

She could only imagine the name he'd choose. Two could play that game. Vanessa tapped in her number and handed the phone back. "I'll wait for your text. I should get up to the bride."

Topher rolled his eyes.

Vanessa narrowed her gaze and poked her finger into his chest with each word. "Don't. Touch. The. Flowers."

Irritating, annoying, obnoxious, interfering, insulting, aggravating man.

That was the only reason he made her pulse race.

It had nothing to do with his sea green eyes and broad shoulders.

Not. One. Thing.

VANESSA FISHER SURVEYED the tall urns of flowers spaced evenly down the grand staircase at Peacock Hill. Everything here, at least, was in place. She turned on the bottom step and ran her gaze over the small seating area set up in the foyer. The central aisle followed the stairs and would lead Azure Hewitt from her impressive entrance to her waiting groom.

Vanessa choked off a wistful sigh.

She was content.

Ish.

Okay, not at all. But florists did a lot of wedding flowers, so she couldn't let on that the only thing in life she wanted more than to get married was to get her dad off her back. How much did her father pushing her to find a husband factor in to her desire to wed? No way to tell.

She pulled her phone out of the pocket of her pantsuit and snapped a couple of photos of the room.

Vanessa glanced over her shoulder at the stairs. It was no wonder Azure had chosen inside for the ceremony. She probably wouldn't pass up that staircase either—talk about an entrance. Plus it was nine zillion degrees outside with enough humidity that by rights it should be raining. That was the downside of Labor Day weekend. People might celebrate it as the end of summer, but summer weather held on for another solid six weeks. Minimum.

Bride. Time to focus on the bride.

Vanessa turned her back on the seating and climbed the stairs to the second floor. The giggling that echoed down the hall made it easy to determine where Azure and her attendants were gathered to dress. She ducked into the small room just off the stairs where she'd stashed the cooler holding the bouquets.

Flowers in hand, she knocked on the door.

Azureopened the door, laughing. She looked resplendent in her white dress—though trailing lines of color immediately drew Vanessa's eye. Tiny flowers embroidered in bright colors on the bodice flowed down onto the skirt where beads and sequins embellished them. It was an unusual departure from the standard white dress, but somehow it suited Azure.

"Oh, flowers! Aren't they fun?" Azure reached for her bridal bouquet. "I love it. It's even better than the sketch."

"I'm glad you like it. Hopefully that will continue as you see everything else." Vanessa peered into the room. "Is everyone else ready for theirs?"

"Of course. Come in." Azure picked up her skirts with one hand and bustled back into the room. "Flowers are here."

Vanessa worked to remember who was who as she distributed the attendant bouquets. Deidre was easy. She was the tiny, pixie-like blonde sporting the beginnings of a baby bump. Of course, Vanessa only knew it was a baby instead of too many candy bars because the woman went out of her way to mention her pregnancy in every conversation.

"These are lovely." Claire buried her nose in the tight knot of blooms. "And they smell good, too. I understand why we're starting to see more of you around here for weddings."

"They really do look great." Sean stepped through the door. "Everyone ready?"

Azure turned. "Is it time? I feel like it should be time."

Sean laughed.

Vanessa's heart ached. What would it be like to be just minutes away from walking down the aisle toward the man she loved? Or any man, for that matter? Someone she loved would, of course, be ideal, but she could settle for someone willing. Especially if he hurried up and made that willingness known.

"Just about. Does it help to know Matt's as anxious as you are?" Sean fished his phone from his pocket and frowned at the display before tapping. "Sorry."

"Problem?" Azure's face clouded.

"Not at all. Just some antsy guests who already claimed seats. Why don't I go signal the string quartet and we can get everyone seated? The photographer said she'd finished all the pre-ceremony shots we had planned."

Azure nodded.

"Great. You've got everything set, right, Vanessa?" Sean turned to hold Vanessa's gaze.

A smile seemed the safest response. Everything up here was fine. The men had their boutonnieres. The cake tent was another story.

Sean frowned and inched closer, lowering his voice. "No word from Topher yet?"

"Not yet. It's only been, what, twenty minutes? How long does he need?"

"That's a good question. Look, why don't you head back out? He has to have something completely finished. You can dress the tables behind him. Be nice."

Be nice? "I'm always nice."

Sean closed his eyes. Vanessa imagined him counting to ten. He did a lot of that when she was around. She didn't mean to cause him anxiety—for a long time she'd hoped Sean might be the guy she could talk to about her own wedding problem. Dating him wouldn't have been a hardship. That had been squashed this past spring. Sean and Larissa weren't engaged yet, but they might as well be. Vanessa could practically see little cartoon hearts circling their heads when they were together.

"Just try a little harder, okay?"

"Did you tell *him* that?"

Sean sighed. "As a matter of fact, yes."

Vanessa dipped her chin. Good enough. If Topher could pull it together, so could she.

2

Topher set the last of the pre-plated desserts on their table and stood back. All the dishes marched in ruler-straight lines. Crisp. Clean.

Perfect.

All that was left was the cake. Not that setting that up was a snap. He could probably text Vanessa. She could dress the two tables he'd finished. Except the woman could talk. She was never silent. She probably talked in her sleep—not that he was volunteering to ever find that out. Topher fought a shudder. Who in his right mind would sign up to marry her?

Maybe that was unfair.

She was cute. Not model-gorgeous, but then, what woman really was? It wasn't as if she'd send small children screaming for their mommies.

But her voice.

Topher carefully drew the base layer of the three-tiered wedding cake from its protective cocoon inside the cooler and set it on the center table. He nudged it until it occupied the exact middle of the space then walked around the table to ensure it looked right from all sides. Satisfied, he checked the stability of the dowels he'd inserted before leaving the bakery and reached into the cooler for the second tier.

"Were you going to let me know I could start in here before or after the wedding was finished?"

Topher glanced over the table and frowned. Vanessa stood just inside the tent, arms crossed, her usual scowl etched into her features. So much for finishing in silence. "Slipped my mind."

"I guess it's a good thing Sean's more aware of time. I can start on these tables, right?"

"Right." Sean was going to be annoyed. Rightfully. Topher turned back to the second tier of cake. He owed his friend an apology. Vanessa too? Man, did he? That stuck in his throat like a too-big bite of steak. Abandoning the cake, he stood. "I'm sorry I forgot to text."

Vanessa turned, eyebrows raised. She studied him for a moment before nodding slowly. "Thanks. I'll try not to be in your way."

He watched her turn back to arranging flowers and petals among the dessert plates. She was detail oriented, he'd give her that. And a good florist, for that matter. Even though it had galled him, he'd sent a few clients her way when they were struggling to come up with someone to do their flowers. For all her faults, Vanessa always came through.

Topher returned to the cake. If the ceremony was starting already, he needed to get a move on. It wasn't simply a matter of tossing three tiers on top of one another, no matter how easy the TV shows made it look.

When he finished making minute adjustments to the final tier, Topher arched his back, pressing his fists into his aching muscles.

"It looks great. What else goes on this table?"

Right. Vanessa. Amazingly, she'd managed to stay quiet

while he assembled the cake. Or he'd finally found a way to tune her out. He reached into his cooler for a bottle of water and took a long drink before answering. "Just your flowers. They didn't even want a discreet stack of plates to make serving easier, so I'm storing them below. It'd be good if you could leave space for them to move up when it's time."

"I can do that. The cake needs to be the centerpiece here. I don't think we need to add much to finish dressing the table."

Topher's phone buzzed. An echoing chime sounded across the tent. "That's Sean. They're doing the final prayer and getting ready for the reception. Are you set in the serving area and tables?"

Vanessa nodded.

"I'll let him know. Can I help with this at all?"

"I've got it. It won't take long—actually, could you grab that empty box?" Vanessa gestured vaguely behind her. "Move it somewhere it won't be visible while I finish here?"

"Sure." Topher gave the cake a final once-over before texting Sean to let him know everything was nearly set. The ceremony was shorter than he'd anticipated. Or he'd taken longer than usual to set up. Didn't matter. In the end, they'd made it. That was the important thing.

He glanced over and saw Vanessa fiddling with a small spray of flowers in front of the cake. There were two smaller arrangements on the table, one to either side. All of them worked to showcase the cake rather than competing for attention. How did she do it?

Vanessa turned and gave a brisk nod. "Finished."

"Great. Sean says we're welcome to grab food. Want to join me at the back of the line?"

"Yeah, all right."

Why had she hesitated? Because she was difficult. He

couldn't allow himself to forget that. Topher gestured to the tent opening. "After you."

"ENJOY YOUR EVENING." Topher handed the last of the take-home containers of cake to a departing guest and relaxed his facial muscles. Smiling constantly was one of the harder aspects of his job some days.

Sean poked his head through the tent opening. "All set?"

"Yeah. Breakdown shouldn't take long. I'll be out of your hair in thirty, unless you need me to help with everything out there?" Please say no. He'd spent entirely too much time around Vanessa today. The only thing he wanted right now was a quiet drive home and sleep.

"Nah. We've got it. Azure's parents and siblings all pitched in. I guess they're hanging around Peacock Hill for a few days as an impromptu family reunion since it's rare for them to all be in the same place."

"Seems like a nice family, although her parents are . . ."

"Odd. The word you're looking for is odd." Sean shrugged. "They're not the strangest I've encountered in my life. But they're up there. Azure was saying there's some tension because she and Cyan—did you meet him?" At Topher's nod, Sean continued, "The two of them became Christians and their dad is seriously unhappy about it."

"That's too bad." Topher's parents had raised him in church, so it was strange to imagine not having that upbringing. Not that they'd taken it beyond a couple hours once a week, but those hours at church had laid a foundation. Did his parents know Jesus? Topher didn't have a clear answer. They would say yes. He prayed it was true. "I'll put them on my prayer list."

"I'm doing that, too. Azure's other brother and sisters, too. Indigo especially. I guess her husband disappeared six weeks ago. She's holding strong, but I can't imagine the strain she must be under."

"I'm impressed she made it out here. I think I'd want to be at home in case he turned up." Maybe it was less important in today's world where cell phones meant contact was always possible, but still. How did someone leave home in that situation?

Sean turned as someone called his name then glanced back at Topher. "Gotta run. Let me know if you need help packing up."

Topher shook his head as his friend hurried off. Chances were high that he'd be on the road headed back to Richmond before Sean even had the glimmer of a chance to leave. That's what happened when the full weight of responsibility for an event fell on your shoulders. Topher was content to bring cake and call it a day.

He'd already boxed up the top tier and set it aside for Matt and Azure to save for their one year anniversary. Or, as seemed more likely, to throw away on their one year anniversary. He did his best to wrap the cakes so they would freeze and keep, but there was no way to know. And Topher had no interest in trying year-old cake. Ever.

Packing up was simple. The food had all been eaten or taken home by guests. All that remained was to load up his trays and serving implements. Sean was in charge of the rented plates and dinnerware. He'd seen people shuttling it into the house—presumably to be washed and dried before getting boxed up and returned. Not his problem.

Topher eyed the tables. Normally he'd wipe them down, fold them, and stack them wherever Sean was staging those rentals. Of course Vanessa hadn't said what he ought to do with her flowers first. He drummed his fingers on his leg as he looked around.

The boxes.

He dragged the boxes from under one of the tables and started loading the loose flowers into one of them.

"What are you doing?"

He didn't bother to sigh as he turned. Sure enough, Vanessa was scowling at him from the tent entrance. "Trying to go home."

"I was getting over here as fast as I could. There were a lot of flowers to load back up from the main ceremony area."

"I get that. I hoped it might be helpful. I haven't done anything with the arrangements." Topher offered the box of loose flowers. "This is petals and stuff."

Vanessa took the box and glanced inside. She thawed visibly. "Okay. If you hand me the other box, I'll get these out of your way. Are the tablecloths yours?"

"Yeah. Do you know where Sean is stacking tables?"

Vanessa shook her head.

Always so helpful. Topher grabbed a tablecloth off the nearest table and gave it a snap before folding it and tossing it on top of his coolers. When Vanessa moved away from the other dessert table, he repeated the process.

"Need help with anything?"

"Me?" Topher frowned. Why was she offering to help? "No, I'm good. Thanks."

"Okay. Well. I guess I'll see you around." Vanessa gathered her boxes and headed for the exit.

"Yep." He could think of three upcoming weddings off the top of his head where they'd be thrown together. Again. Of course, if she could keep up the normal façade, maybe they could work together better. Friends didn't seem likely, but was it possible they could get to a point where seeing her name on the vendor list didn't make him die a little inside? He grabbed the last tablecloth and folded it.

"So. Bye."

Topher glanced up. Why hadn't she gone? He gave a tiny wave and turned toward his stack of coolers. There was a canister of disposable disinfecting wipes in there somewhere.

"I was wondering ..."

He found the wipes and stood. "Yeah?"

"Do you do anniversary cakes?"

"Sure. Birthday, anniversary, wedding, just because. I have a bakery in town, you realize that right?"

Red flooded her cheeks. "Actually, no. I thought you just did wedding cakes—maybe out of your home or a rented commercial kitchen."

It wasn't a completely unwarranted assumption. There were people who did that. A lot of them. Wedding cakes were becoming a popular stay-at-home-mom side business. "Ah. Now you know. We make killer éclairs, too."

A ghost of a smile hovered on her lips. "I'll keep that in mind. So—if I wanted to order an anniversary cake?"

"You could call or stop by the shop any time Monday through Saturday between six thirty and five. That's five p.m."

"That's a long day."

"It can be. I have help." He extracted a card from his pocket and held it out. "It's good to have a week's lead time, if that's possible."

"Right. Of course. Thanks." Vanessa tucked the card away and hitched up her boxes. "Later."

He watched her leave and shook his head. That was one weird woman.

3

"Hi, Daddy." Vanessa leaned against the door to her father's office and waited for him to look up from his computer. Everything about the room suited him—the dark wood of the desk and shelves, the leather chairs, even the state-of-the-art electronics managed to fit the space—it all screamed important man of business, disturb at your own risk.

"Vanessa." Dad took off the half-moon readers he'd grudgingly started wearing while working at the computer and studied her. "You look casual."

"It's a Labor Day barbecue, Dad. I didn't think black tie was even optional."

"Yes, well, you know how your mother feels about jeans."

She couldn't stop herself from glancing down. She'd worn black jeans. They looked like dress pants from a distance. It was like her parents had denim radar. "Is she going to give me the clothing of the poor speech again?"

Her dad's lips twitched. "More than likely. I don't imagine you brought something more suitable?"

She sighed. "I have linen capris in the car."

"Good girl. Go change before your mother sees you. Then

you can come back and tell me how your little flower shop is going."

There was no point in being offended. Or annoyed. This was just how Dad was. He didn't mean anything by it. Vanessa forced a smile and repeated that to herself. "Sure. Be right back."

"Changing, Miss Vanessa?" Estelle, the housekeeper-slash-cook-slash-nanny appeared seemingly out of thin air as Vanessa crossed the foyer toward the front door.

"You knew I'd have to."

"So did you." Estelle's eyes twinkled. "I'm not sure why you keep trying."

"Because I'm almost thirty. It seems like I ought to be able to dress myself." Vanessa tugged open the heavy, solid wood door and trotted down the path to her car. At least she'd convinced her parents to let her park in the circular drive instead of them sending someone out to move her vehicle every time she arrived. It was better to be primed for a quick getaway. Just in case. She grabbed the spare outfit from the backseat of her modest, second-hand sedan—another point of contention between her and her parents—and hurried back to the house. No point keeping Estelle from her duties any longer than necessary.

"You go on and change now. If you leave your jeans in the powder room, I'll see they're returned to your car."

"You don't have to do that."

Estelle smiled. "Your father's waiting."

Right. To talk about her business. Even though he was never going to admit she was making a success of it. "Thank you. I don't know how I'd survive here without you."

Estelle chuckled. "I suspect you'd be just fine."

Unlikely. Vanessa ducked into the powder room and made quick work of changing her outfit. She wrinkled her nose at her reflection in the mirror. She looked like a miniature version of her mother now, all dressed up for a casual backyard party. Effortless elegance. That's what Mom tried to drum into Vanessa's head. She wriggled her shoulders against the itchy fabric in the blouse. Uncomfortable elegance was more like it. Just once, she'd like to wear jeans and a t-shirt to a party. Or, heaven help them all, shorts.

Scandalous.

She folded her clothes and set them neatly on the shelf of the bathroom organizer. Estelle would get them out of the way before Mom could see them and, in so doing, save Vanessa's bacon. She'd have to remember to send a little flower arrangement as a thank you. If she remembered right, Estelle loved hot pink gerbera daisies—and Vanessa had the perfect ones in stock.

"There you are, darling." Her mother's apprising gaze took her in from head to toe. "Don't you look fresh and cool."

Vanessa's spine stiffened. She tried to relax her shoulders so her mother wouldn't ask what was wrong. There was no need to get into it. Mom would deny she'd meant anything by it and insist Vanessa was being over sensitive. "Thanks, Mom. It's good to see you."

"I'm glad you could come. I worried you'd take on a last minute wedding to get out of it. Your father has some important business contacts coming this afternoon and he wants to show you off."

For some unknown reason.

Her mother didn't finish with those words, but Vanessa heard them anyway. "I'm not sure I can stay all evening."

Her mother waved that idea away. "Of course you can. In fact, I'll have Estelle make sure your suite is set up and you can stay the night. I don't understand why you insist on living in that tiny apartment over your little flower shop."

"I can't stay the night, Mom. It's nearly three hours back

home. I can stay until eight, okay?" Even that was going to have her dragging tomorrow, but it was worth it if it kept her parents happy. She didn't need them deciding to adjust the terms of her trust any more than they already had. "Dad wanted to talk to me about my business."

"Oh, of course. Go see your father. I'll check that the kitchen has everything under control. Before you go, I'd like to talk to you about flowers for a few events we're planning around the Gold Cup next year."

"Isn't that in May? There's plenty of time."

A tiny furrow formed between her mother's eyebrows. "The job isn't yours yet. I have to convince the committee you're capable of handling something so far away. As you said, it's close to three hours and we do have florists locally."

"Why don't you have the committee send me the bid information and I'll look it over. May can be busy for me." She didn't need her mother drumming up business or elbowing aside companies who counted on these events for their own budgets. Healthy competition was one thing. Nepotism another. If she'd wanted to run her business on her parents' terms, she would have started it in Winchester.

Her mother sighed. "If that's what you want. I don't see why you can't simply appreciate that I'm trying to help you."

Vanessa leaned in and kissed her mother's cheek. "I do appreciate it, Mom, but my business is doing fine. If you're not convinced, why don't you sit in with Dad and me while we go over it?"

"No, that's fine. Tell your father we're expecting the first of his guests by four so he needs to be ready."

"Okay. I love you, Mom."

Her mom offered a small smile before disappearing down the corridor toward the kitchen. Vanessa blew out a breath and shook her arms to loosen her tense muscles. Now to face her father's disapproval and subtle digs about her chosen profession. Her mom had let her off light, all things considered. Maybe Dad would keep up the trend.

HER HEAD THROBBED in time with the windshield wipers. The rain had started when she was half-way home, and it was as if it unlocked all the pressure that had built up during her visit to her parents. Vanessa gripped the steering wheel. Almost home.

She'd take medicine, climb into bed, and completely ignore the fact that she needed to be up to receive and process a flower order in—she glanced at the dashboard clock—just about seven hours.

That was her own fault.

She'd tried to leave at seven. Then again at eight. Finally, a little after nine, when all but one of her parents' friends had left, Vanessa had managed to convince her mom that yes, really, she needed to get home. And so she'd disappointed them.

Again.

Vanessa pulled into the lot behind her building and shifted into park. She frowned at the only other car there—a rusted heap that didn't look like it could run if it wanted to. Great. Now she'd have to call a tow truck and wait up for that to be taken care of. She'd learned better than to let it ride until morning. The first year she'd been in business people were used to the building being empty. They'd drop their cars in the lot and catch a taxi to the airport, taking the chance that free parking—even unsecured—was better than paying what they'd be charged in the economy lot. And then her customers couldn't find a space and would go to the florist six miles away in a strip mall with ample parking. Even though those people didn't know a daisy from a rose.

The pain in her head surged. Aspirin first. Tow truck second.

Vanessa pushed open her car door, grabbed her purse, and made a dash for the semi-sheltered doorway that hid stairs to her apartment over the shop. She climbed up, head pounding, and fumbled for her keys. She nearly tripped over the man's legs.

Vanessa clamped off the scream and started to back away, her heart thundering.

"Nessa?" The man shifted and her brother's face, hidden by a scraggly beard, peeked up at her.

"James?" She pinched the bridge of her nose and willed herself to think over her banging head. There were a thousand questions. Most of them didn't matter in the overall scheme. Her brief fantasy of falling into bed and sleeping off the headache disappeared as she struggled to keep things casual. Her brother hated when people fussed. "Come on in. I'll make coffee. Is that your car down there?"

He nodded and shuffled to his feet.

Vanessa unlocked the apartment door. Well, at least she didn't have to call a tow.

She dropped her purse and keys on the small table by the door and kicked her sandals under it. "Make yourself at home. The bathroom's down the hall on the right if you want to wash up. Want some eggs?"

He smiled and Vanessa could pick out little pieces of the brother she remembered in his expression. "You always made the best midnight eggs. You don't mind?"

"Of course not." What was she going to do? Kick him to the curb? He was the only brother—the only sibling—she had. Even if he was responsible for a lot of how Mom and Dad treated her.

"Can I take a shower?" James shed his ratty coat and draped it over the arm of her couch, clutching a small duffel.

"If you want, of course."

He nodded once before disappearing down the hall.

First things first. Vanessa shook two pain relievers into her hand, considered a moment, and added a third. She filled a glass at the sink and downed them before turning to her coffee setup. She ground beans and got the machine going then opened her fridge. She'd offered the eggs before thinking. There should be a couple in there, but what she had that could go alongside them was a question she couldn't answer off the top of her head.

A quick rummage produced a full carton of eggs, a slightly squishy tomato, and the tail end of a block of cheddar. Good enough. She had bread—sandwiches were her go-to meal most days—so she could round things out with toast. Her brother had looked gaunt. When was the last time he'd had a reasonable meal?

Five years. Most of the anger was gone, but little tendrils of it still popped up occasionally. Still, now that her parents' full attention rested on her, she almost understood the desire to run and not leave a forwarding address. Hadn't she moved just about as far away as she could while still staying in state? Besides, none of that mattered in the overall scheme of things. Her brother was back. She wasn't going to push him away with her reaction.

By the time he emerged, beard trimmed and wet hair neatly combed, Vanessa had two plates of scrambled eggs, a broiled tomato, toast, and two mugs of coffee set out on her kitchen table.

"Smells good. Do you have a washing machine?"

Vanessa nodded. "After you eat, okay? Cold eggs are gross."

"You were always pickier than me." But James pulled out a chair and sat. He reached for his fork.

Vanessa cleared her throat and offered her hand.

"Right. Sorry." James took her fingers in his and licked his lips. "Why don't you? It's been awhile."

Vanessa studied her older brother before bowing her head and offering a short prayer of thanks for the food and her brother's visit. Silently she tacked on a plea for wisdom and the right words, because it was clear she was going to need both. "So."

He forked up a big bite and paused with the food at his lips. "So?"

"Come on, James."

"I'm not sure I want to bare my soul if you're going to call me that." Hurt mixed with a hint of resignation in his eyes.

The meager walls around her heart crumbled. He was her brother. For good or ill. "Jamie."

His grin flashed, revealing a hint of the boy she grew up with before disappearing back into this man she hardly recognized. "Better."

Vanessa focused on her eggs, waiting for him to speak.

He didn't.

She scraped up her last bite of egg. "I'm forced to repeat myself. So?"

"Right." He pushed his empty plate toward the middle of the table and tented his hands. "What first? Where have I been? Why haven't I called? Emailed? Texted? Sent up smoke signals?"

"Basically, yes. I was worried, Jamie. Mom and Dad were, too."

He snorted. "You, I buy. Them? Nah. I burned that bridge well enough it's not getting rebuilt."

She opened her mouth to object but snapped it shut. Dad was liable to forgive him, after some appropriate groveling. But Mom? This was more than trying to wear jeans to a garden party. "We'll see. Don't sell God short."

"Oh, right." Sarcasm dripped from his words. "Trust me, Nessa, God has no use for me."

"Jamie. What happened to you?" This wasn't the brother she

knew. "You disappeared five years ago when you got the second tier of your trust. Where did you go?"

"Where didn't I go? I started in Europe. I'd planned to start a business with some college friends. We gave it a go—sort of." Jamie stroked his beard. "We parted ways and I drifted. Then the money ran out. I had enough to get back to the states, and I've just been sort of wandering, I guess."

"The money ran out? Your trust? How is that possible?" He'd had access to just under five million dollars. The same amount was due her, if she could meet the new terms of the trust. That seemed unlikely right now.

"The business ate up a lot of it. We set up a moped rental in Greece, thinking tourists would flock. It wasn't as easy as it sounded on paper. After the second month, we weren't getting along. Then Rod took off with six of the bikes and all the petty cash. There was no recovery. We sold off, as best we could, but Kenny insisted that money was his—back pay owed. I didn't fight it. I still had what I thought would be enough. But we were raised to travel in style, you know?"

She nodded. She did know. Her choice to live above her shop and drive a reasonable car didn't sit well with either of her parents, though Dad was a tiny bit less critical. "You're back now though, right?"

"I don't know."

"What do you mean you don't know? Jamie, you have to stay. Mom and Dad—"

"Leave them out of this."

"But—"

Jamie shook his head. "If you call them, I'm gone. It's not so bad being homeless."

"Sure, now. What are you going to do in winter?"

He shrugged. "Travel south, I guess. I can pick up work when

I need a little money. Panhandle. Some days on a street corner I make enough to spring for a decent hotel."

"Jamie." Her mind raced through options. Everything in her wanted to call her parents. They didn't talk about her brother often, but his disappearance had shaken them. It had shaken the foundation of their marriage. They needed to know. Maybe later. "A job."

"What?" Jamie turned from his study of her stove.

Vanessa frowned. "Do you want some more?"

He managed a sheepish look. "I didn't really eat today."

She stood and took her plate to the sink before getting out more eggs. "They'll have to be plain this time. I'd planned to hit the market but it didn't happen."

"That's fine. I appreciate this."

"Come work for me." Vanessa dropped bread into her toaster before cracking the first egg into a bowl.

"I can't—doing what?"

That was the million dollar question, wasn't it? "You can count, right? And you still have a driver's license?"

He nodded.

She stirred the eggs into the hot skillet and let them sit a moment before moving them around. "You can help with inventory and deliveries until you figure out what you want to do. You have an MBA from one of the top Ivy League schools. It shouldn't take you too long to find a job you actually want."

Jamie blew out a breath and stared at his plate as she scooted the eggs onto it.

She collected the toast and set it on the side before resuming her seat. "What do you think?"

"They're delicious, thank you."

Despite herself, Vanessa laughed. She punched his arm. "About the job, Jamie."

"It sounds like a place to start. But I can't promise to stay forever."

Her heart sank. She wanted him here. Or at least in Virginia. Somewhere they could get together now and then and try to restore the camaraderie they'd had as kids. But she'd settle for short term if it was all he could offer right now. "Just promise if you decide to go, you won't leave without saying goodbye this time."

4

Topher unbuttoned his chef's coat as he plodded up the short flight of stairs from his van to his townhouse. Why had he agreed to cater a rehearsal dinner when he had a morning wedding the next day? His thoughts flashed to the stack of invoices waiting for him to have a paperwork day. Right. That would be why.

His steps faltered when his gaze landed on the silhouette of someone sitting propped against his front door.

"You should leave your porch light on. Or get one of those daylight timer things."

"Brian?"

"I tried to call. Figured showing up would be okay."

"Yeah. Of course, man. Have you been waiting long?"

Brian heaved to his feet and shrugged. "It's a nice night. Not raining."

That was true enough, though there was enough humidity in the air it might as well be. Topher unlocked the door and pushed it open. "Come in out of the heat. Dave couldn't come?"

Brian held Topher's gaze as he stepped past him. "He's on a date."

"A . . . oh." What was he supposed to do with that? He'd been friends with Brian since elementary school and, while he didn't approve of his friend's lifestyle, he still loved him. It had to hurt a lot to be in a place where his fiancé was on a date with someone else. Topher kicked his shoes off and aimed them toward the credenza just inside the door. He tossed his coat at the top of it, dropped his keys in the fancy wooden bowl his mother had given him as a housewarming gift, and went up the two steps to the main level of his townhome. Veering right into the kitchen, he aimed for the fridge. "Want a drink?"

"I don't suppose you have a beer in there."

"I do if you don't mind a 'root' in front of it."

"Yeah, why not." Brian headed toward the living room and flopped onto the sofa. "Can I crash here tonight?"

"It's that bad?"

"Did you miss the part where he's on a date?" Brian took the root beer and twisted the cap off the bottle.

Topher settled on the other end of the couch and opened his own bottle. "I was kind of hoping I'd misheard. Of course you can stay here as long as you like. How did this even happen?"

"Not sure. We were hammering out a few more wedding details over dinner and I got upset that he wanted to change the music. Again. I mean, come on. We've beaten that horse to death and finally had something we both agreed on. Or so I thought. He got nasty. I might have responded in kind. Next thing I know he's grabbing his cell phone and making a date on his way out the door."

"Sorry. That's awful. No chance you misunderstood who he was calling?"

Brian shook his head. "I don't see how. He stopped seeing Alejandro when we got serious."

"They're not friends?"

"Never were. Dave used to say there was only one good thing about Alejandro."

Topher winced and held up a hand. "I don't need to know. So you'll stay here until you work things out with him. There's time."

Brian drained his root beer, leaned forward and set the bottle on the glass coffee table. "How are you this optimistic? Seriously. There's no working things out. If the woman you were engaged to hooked up with her ex, you'd find a way to work things out?"

"I don't know. Maybe? Forgiveness is a thing."

"That's you and your Jesus nonsense talking." Brian held up a finger and looked away for a minute. "Sorry. Out of line. Yes, in theory, forgiveness is a thing. I'm going to hold out for karma biting him in the rear. I just hope I'm there to see it."

Topher hid a smile behind his bottle. "I will admit that's probably the first thing I'd feel given the situation. It's a betrayal, man. I know it's gotta sting."

"But?"

"I don't know. I'm gonna stick with I'm sorry and stop there. What do you want me to say when he calls?"

"He won't call."

Topher was willing to put money on it, and he wasn't a gambler. Dave was going to call. Dave called when Brian took too long at the grocery store. "You know he thinks I'm after you. Even though he knows I'm straight."

Brian snorted. "I guess I played right into that, coming here. Sorry, man."

Topher shrugged. "I don't care unless it's going to cause problems for you down the road."

"I don't see how. Where else am I going to go? My parents'?"

"They're still angry?"

"That's one way of putting it. Right now, I'm convinced if someone asked them, they'd deny ever having a boy."

"Sorry." Topher frowned. He didn't understand parents who turned their back on a child. No matter the reason.

"Anyway, I appreciate you taking me in. Tell me if you need me to find somewhere else. I'll understand if your girlfriend isn't on board."

"What girlfriend?" Topher laughed. "No such luck, man."

"Yeah, well, I guess I was hoping someone was having some luck in love these days. Besides, I thought I heard you were seeing a florist or something? Someone you do a lot of weddings with anyway."

Topher snorted. "No. The only florist I've been seeing regularly is Vanessa Fisher. And believe me, there is no chance I will ever date her."

"She's a troll?"

"What? No. She's fine. Nice looking, even. Just . . ." Topher hesitated. What was it about Vanessa that rubbed him the wrong way? Besides everything. "She's just always in my way."

Brian grinned.

"What?"

"Nothing."

"Don't say 'nothing' in that tone. I know what you're thinking and that's not happening."

Brian lifted his hands. "Hey. I didn't say a thing."

"Whatever. You need me to show you around, point out the guest room, or should we put on a movie?"

"Lots of explosions, no romance."

"That I can do." Topher fished the remote out from between the couch cushions and turned on the enormous flat screen across the room. He scrolled through his digital movie library and hit play when he found something that would fit the bill. No romance. That was a sentiment he could get behind. Especially when it came to Vanessa.

She was *not* the woman for him.

TOPHER CROSSED THE FOYER, weaving between the small clumps of people on his way to the worship center. He wasn't a first-time visitor, but it was still a relatively new church for him. Several conversations over the last year—most of them with Sean Fitzgerald, wedding planner extraordinaire—had convinced Topher to look around a little. He wasn't church shopping, exactly, but he needed something that made his walk with God feel more like a relationship and less like a box to check off each week.

Maybe that was up to him more than the church he attended.

"Hey, man." Sean grinned when Topher turned. "Fancy meeting you here."

"Yeah, well, you said to try new churches. This is actually my third week. Where've you been?"

Sean laughed. "Touché. We were trying Larissa's old church. She really wants to keep going there, but . . . I don't know."

"Poor you."

"Yeah, yeah, I know. Still. Neither of us have history here, so she's more open to giving it a shot."

Topher scanned the crowd. "Where is she?"

"Coffee." Sean pointed in the direction Topher remembered seeing refreshments set up. "Here she comes."

"Sean, look who I found—oh, hey Topher." Larissa grinned. "Maybe this is a good place after all. You remember Vanessa, right?"

Vanessa giggled. "Since we saw each other yesterday at the Chandler wedding, I imagine they do."

Topher froze. That giggle. Didn't she know it was horrible? Brain-melting, even? He forced a smile. "Good to see you."

"There you are." A man slipped up behind Vanessa and dropped his hand on her shoulder. "Found friends, I see?"

Vanessa looked up at the guy, love practically beaming out of her eyes.

Topher's gut clenched. He frowned unable to concentrate on the words Vanessa was continuing to say. So she had a boyfriend. This was good. And the guy was—scrawny. Tall, sure, and maybe if he filled out some he'd be buff, but Topher could totally take him. Not that he was going to be fighting for Vanessa's affections. The guy just wasn't what Topher pictured when he imagined the kind of guy she'd sink her claws into.

" . . . Jamie. Jamie, Sean—I talked about him a little, remember? His fiancée, Larissa—"

"Girlfriend." Larissa jabbed Sean in the side with her elbow. "There's been no proposal."

Sean mumbled something, his face reddening.

"I'm Topher." Better to tune in and maybe get his friend out of the hot seat for a little bit. "How'd you meet Vanessa?"

A smile flickered at the corner of Jamie's lips before it was smothered by the guy's beard. "My parents."

"Oh. Family connections are good." Topher cleared his throat. "I'm going to grab a seat. It was good to run into you all."

Vanessa shot Jamie a puzzled look.

Topher hurried off. No need to explore that any further. His stomach was still tight and rolling. Was he coming down with something? Maybe he should head home. It had to be the flu. Or food poisoning.

Because there was no way he was jealous of a guy who was dating Vanessa.

5

Rude, abrupt man. She scowled after Topher's retreating back. "Excuse him. He's always that way. I swear he never learned any manners."

Sean's eyebrows lifted. "That's not Topher at all, though I'll admit he's being weird today."

"Of course you take his side. Have you forgotten, oh let's see, every wedding I've been at ever?"

Larissa snickered.

"I . . . okay, but you get in his space—"

"Just stop. He's your friend, I get it. You'll defend him to the last, but let's be clear, I think he's a jerk, and his behavior backs that up." Vanessa huffed out a breath and glanced at her brother. "You want to go grab seats?"

Larissa reached out and grabbed Vanessa's arm. "Sit with us. I promise no one will defend Topher."

Sean opened his mouth but snapped it shut when Larissa glared.

"Works for me. I don't even care if we sit with that guy. Anyone who gets my sister's blood up that fast is fascinating.

She's usually pretty even-keeled." Jamie studied Vanessa. "Why do you let him get under your skin?"

"Let?" Vanessa clamped her lips closed on the argument that threatened to bubble up. That man. Why couldn't she control herself around him? "I'm working on it."

Jamie leaned close and whispered in her ear. "I think he got the impression you and I are an item."

Vanessa snorted. "Even if he did—which is dumb, since I introduced you as my brother—why would he care?"

"Just sayin'. Dude looked like he took a fist to the gut."

"You're way off base. You're so off base you might as well be playing football." She took a deliberate breath and turned her attention back to Sean and Larissa. "Do you have a preference about where we sit?"

"I'm going to want to talk to you about this later." Larissa's sly smile made it clear she'd heard the whole of the conversation between Vanessa and Jamie.

"There's nothing to talk about. My brother is an imbecile. The last relationship he had was how long ago now? Ten years?" Vanessa smoothed her skirt and started walking toward the worship center doors. There was nothing there. Topher was a jerk and she, well she'd hold off on saying she hated him, but it came close. And he returned the feeling.

Jealous.

Vanessa snorted again.

Living on the street had clearly impaired her brother's mental function.

"You up for a little drive?" Vanessa collected her Bible and pocketbook from beneath her seat and stood as the congregation began milling toward the door.

Jamie shrugged. "I'm at your disposal. Why?"

"I have an idea." She bit her lip. Maybe she should call or email first. Except it was a nice afternoon for a drive and she didn't want to spend more time cooped up in her apartment with her brother watching TV. She loved him.

But he was aimless.

One week in and it was already starting to get annoying.

She liked her space. And quiet.

"It's a nice day for it. You didn't want to grab lunch with them?" He jerked his thumb at Sean and Larissa, who were making their way toward the door.

Vanessa followed his gaze and shook her head. They were on an intersecting course with Topher. They'd invite him, too. He'd probably agree because it was unlikely the man had more than one friend. Which would mean more time around the guy trying to keep from morphing into Mom at her snootiest. She hated when Mom got that way. Hearing her own voice come out like that was unbearable.

She couldn't seem to stop it.

"We'll drive through somewhere. Get a burger."

Jamie pressed his hand to her forehead.

Vanessa jerked back and hissed, "What are you doing?"

"Checking for fever. You don't eat fast food. Ever. Not since you were what, nine?"

"I do, too." Sort of. Did sub shops count as fast food? Just because they were a little healthier didn't make them any less convenient. "Maybe not routinely, but it happens."

"Uh-huh. When was the last time you had a french fry. Snobby shoestring potatoes at a sit down restaurant don't count." Jamie held open the door to the foyer.

She wrinkled her nose. "I might've had fast food without succumbing to french fries."

"Why? They're the best part."

Her brother sounded genuinely appalled and Vanessa had to laugh. "Maybe if you're a man with a teenager's metabolism. Some of us have to work to avoid putting on extra weight."

"You sound like Mom."

She winced. "I do not."

"Trust me." He angled his head and pulled open the door to the parking lot. "Why is that? Practicing for when your trust kicks in? Gonna pitch it all and live like a lady of the manor?"

Vanessa stiffened. She'd avoided every mention of her trust that her brother flung at her, but it was getting old. She turned and parked her hands on her hips. "I may not get my trust, thank you very much. So no, I'm not counting on that. And I don't sound like Mom."

"Touchy." Jamie slid into the passenger seat and reached for his seatbelt. "Why wouldn't you get your money? You'll be thirty in what, three months?"

"Five. February, remember? Mom's December." It was like he was trying to push her buttons.

"Right, sorry." He flashed a toothy grin. "Pretty sure you have to be in jail to not get your money. Even then, I'm not positive the terms would completely prohibit it."

"Your terms, maybe. My terms? They got a lot stricter." Vanessa shifted into drive and pulled out into the slowly moving line of cars leaving the church parking lot. That was all she planned to say about that. She wasn't going to add to the guilt her brother was obviously carrying around. "Do you have a drive-through preference?"

Jamie frowned at her before shaking his head. "Not really. But the golden arches are a classic for a reason."

Ugh. Of course he picked that one. She'd asked. At least there was one on practically every corner, so they could get a little away from church and head toward the highway. Maybe it'd be less congested.

"Where are we going?"

"Peacock Hill."

"The wedding venue thing? You don't have a job today, do you? Working on Sunday's rough even for me."

"Yes, the wedding venue. No, no job. Just some people I'd like you to meet."

"People you'd like me to meet. You're not secretly checking me into rehab, are you? Because I promise, I'm clean. Drugs were never my thing."

"That's good to know. It's not rehab. It's Peacock Hill and a group of people who I think are interesting. Maybe we'd both do well to get to know them better." She'd developed a bit of a friendship with Claire over the last six months. The woman was smart and funny. Single. Normally her relationship wouldn't matter, but Vanessa was growing tired of wading through boyfriends, fiancés and husbands to get to her girlfriends. It was her age. Of course it was. Thirty was looming for most of her friends—or it had already snuck by—and suddenly biological clocks were ticking louder than anyone's desire to have a fulfilling career.

Seemed like the ladies at Peacock Hill—and their men—understood it was possible to balance both. Hard, maybe. But possible.

"All right. Tell me about them."

Vanessa filled the rest of the drive with anecdotes about the people at Peacock Hill. Her brother laughed as she described pixie-like Deidre who could wield a hammer like a Norse god—even when she was expecting—and how she'd taken everything she had and invested it into the ramshackle mansion and turned it into a glamorous destination with which not even their mom would be able to find fault.

Before long, they were turning onto the long driveway that curved up to the house. Jamie let out a low whistle. "I thought you were joking when you called it a mansion. Does Mom know this is here?"

"Of course. She's already trying to figure out how to work it to her advantage that I know the people who own it. So far the fact that it's all the way down here is working against her. I'm hoping to keep it that way."

Jamie snickered. "Good luck with that."

Her brother was probably right. Didn't mean Vanessa had any intention of trying to get her mother down here. Ever.

"I thought you said there was no event today."

Vanessa scanned the cars parked in front of the mansion. Most of them were semi-familiar. "I think it might just be the folks who live and work here. They get together to hang out a lot."

"Huh. That's a lot of people."

She nodded and eased her car behind a vintage pickup—was it Azure's? That seemed right. "Come on, they're nice."

"Since when are you a joiner?"

That put a hitch in her stride. Vanessa paused and studied her brother. "Since I realized I'm on my own. I got the first drip when I graduated, just like you. And, just like you, I set it up as a charitable foundation."

Jamie held up his hands. "That's what's expected. Don't blame me for that."

Vanessa closed her eyes and counted to ten. She tried to hold back the words, but they slipped out anyway, "Right. You're right. And when I didn't realize it was the only money I'd ever get, it made sense."

He frowned. "Don't be ridiculous. You're almost to your thirtieth. If the shop's in trouble, you can hang on a few more months, right?"

"That's how it used to work. Then you went off on your little spree, and Mom and Dad changed things. Now, if I'm not engaged to a suitable prospect by my thirtieth birthday, all future trust distributions are funneled directly into the charity I set up with the first."

"They—that—how—" Jamie's shoulders fell and his voice dropped to a whisper, "I'm sorry."

Vanessa nodded. "I wasn't going to say anything. I'm okay. My shop is holding its own. I'm not counting on the money for living expenses. At the same time? I'm not opposed to finding someone. Maybe Dad's timeframe is speeding up how I would've gone about it, but it's not all bad."

"There's someone here you're interested in?"

"Oh. No. Everyone here is spoken for."

"Then I guess I'm still confused."

She sighed. "Friends, Jamie. Friends make it all a little more bearable."

"Until they stab you in the back."

"Maybe. But then, I don't have money. No one even knows about the money. So I think—at least I hope—they like me for who I am."

Jamie threw his arm across her shoulders. "They should. You're the real deal, Nessie."

Vanessa shrugged off his arm. "Don't call me that. Unless you like sleeping on the street?"

He laughed. "All right. Introduce me to your friends. They seriously don't know about the money? Who Mom and Dad are?"

"Only Claire, and I swore her to secrecy."

"Why?"

"Because it's nice to know, for once, that I matter simply because I'm me."

6

Topher stood on the steps of Peacock Hill and waved to the couple getting into their car. When they'd started down the driveway, he turned to Sean. "Tell me why I needed to be around for this?"

Sean chuckled. "Because that couple is neurotic and they're insisting every contractor be on board with every decision. So they wanted to be sure you could handle catering at Peacock Hill."

"And I told them—and you—that seeing as how I've worked a number of events here already it wouldn't be a problem."

Sean shrugged. "Customer's always right."

"Unless they aren't." Even he heard the self-pity in his mutter.

"What's going on with you? It's a nice fall day and you said you weren't slammed at the shop, so . . . ?"

Vanessa. That's what was wrong with him. He'd been . . . off since Sunday when he'd seen her with that guy. The skinny, scraggly looking one. What did she see in him? Why did he care? "Nothing."

"Nope. No way. You need to spill it. Let's go in, grab some soda, and take a walk around the lake."

"I should get back to town. We have—" Topher stopped when Sean grabbed his arm.

"Are we friends, Toph?"

He sighed. "You know we are."

"So let's walk."

Fine. He'd walk. But he absolutely wasn't telling Sean about this bizarre and unhealthy fixation on Vanessa. Maybe he had a brain tumor and it was affecting his judgment. "Have I made any strange decisions lately?"

Sean frowned at him as they circled the mansion and headed toward the rear gardens and the lake that lay just beyond. "Not that I know of, why?"

Probably not a tumor then. That would manifest in all areas of his life, wouldn't it? "No reason."

"*What* is going on with you?"

"I can't stop thinking about Vanessa being at church with a guy on Sunday." Topher winced as the words came out. They were ridiculous. He was ridiculous. "Never mind."

"No. No, this is interesting." Sean's eyes glinted with laughter. "You and Vanessa, huh? Larissa called it."

"There isn't any me and Vanessa. Never will be. It might be a brain lesion or something."

Sean stopped and put his hands on his knees as he laughed.

Topher shook his head. "I don't remember giving you a hard time when you fell in love with someone else's fiancée."

Sean took a deep breath and, after a couple of false starts, got his laughter under control. "You're in love with her? That's fast work."

"I didn't say that."

"Didn't you?"

"Absolutely not." He didn't even like the woman. He couldn't possibly be in love with her. That would be insane. "Besides, she's seeing that guy. Jamie. What kind of name is Jamie?"

"It's her brother's name."

Topher snorted. "That's weird. Who goes out with someone who shares the name of their sibling? It's creepy."

"It would be. But Jamie is her brother. Not her boyfriend."

That couldn't be possible. Could it? "Why didn't she introduce him that way?"

"She did. You must've been daydreaming."

Fire crawled up Topher's neck. His ears burned. "Oh, man."

Sean clapped him on the shoulder. "On the positive side, she just figured you were being rude. Again."

"I'm not—"

"You really are when it's Vanessa."

"In my defense, it wasn't long ago you were reminding me how annoyingly lethal her giggle was."

"True. That was when it seemed like she was on a man hunt, and I was in her crosshairs." Sean lifted a shoulder. "Not my finest moment, I'll admit. But she seems to have settled down some since the spring."

Had she? "I haven't noticed."

"Maybe you should."

Topher scrubbed a hand over his face. "Yeah. Maybe I should."

THE SCENT of tomato sauce greeted him as Topher pushed open the door to his townhouse. He kicked off his shoes and glanced over the half-wall into the kitchen. Brian stood at the stove stirring a pot.

"Hi, honey, I'm home."

Brian turned and shook his head. "Funny guy."

"Seemed strangely appropriate." Topher made his way into the kitchen and pulled out a chair at the small table in the bay window. "What're you making?"

"Just spaghetti. For someone who bakes for a living, you don't actually have a whole lot of food in your pantry." Brian tapped the wooden spoon against the side of the pot before resting it on the handle and turning. "How was your day?"

Topher shrugged, trying to ward off the awkwardness of the scene. "Pretty typical. Well, semi-typical. Had a meet with a bride, but she didn't need me there. She's weird—wants everyone to be at every consult so she can be sure the aura's right. Or something like that."

"Not your usual clientele."

"I've had some doozies, but she's definitely near the top of the list. Still, even weirdos get married and want cake."

Brian laughed. "That could be your new slogan."

Topher grinned. "I'll keep it in reserve, just in case. Anyway, that ate up most of the day so I really only checked in at the bakery while they were wrapping up. Looked like they had everything under control, so I left it for Gina to close and headed home."

"Which means you get hot spaghetti instead of reheating something later."

"Appreciate it, man. No word from Dave?"

Brian sighed and turned back toward the stove. "We've had some words."

Topher winced. Not positive ones from the sound of it.

"I can go somewhere else."

"That's not why I asked, Bri. You're welcome here as long as you want to stay. Mi casa and all that. I'm just—"

"What? You're what?" Brian spun to glare at Topher, arms

crossed over his chest. "It's not like you were celebrating Dave's and my relationship with balloons and pennywhistles while it was on."

"I wasn't aware you wanted pennywhistles."

The corners of Brian's mouth twitched. "You know what I mean. You're not as outspoken about it as your friend Sean, but you agree with him, right? That my being gay is a sin."

"Everyone sins, man. I want you to get to know Jesus. That's what I want for you."

"It's always back to Jesus with you, isn't it?"

"Yeah. He's that important. If people end up with nothing to say about me but 'it was always back to Jesus with him' I'll have done it right." Topher blew out a breath. "But what I was going to say was that I'm sorry. Breakups suck. I can only imagine it's worse when you were engaged."

Brian pressed his lips together and gave a curt nod before turning back to the stove. "Get drinks, would you? I'll take one of the flavored seltzer waters you have in the bottom drawer. I swear if I didn't know better, your drink choices would convince me you were the one who preferred men."

Topher snorted and opened the fridge. He grabbed two cans of La Croix. He'd initially bought them when his mom was planning a visit. Then she'd said she was giving up soda—even sparkling water—so he was stuck with them. "They're not that bad."

Brian carried two plates heaping with noodles to the table. "Yes, they are. But if you're not going to stock beer, they'll do."

"If you make a list, I can pick up groceries more in line with your needs." Topher couldn't quite keep the snark out of his tone as he slid a can toward Brian before resuming his seat.

"I'll pick stuff up tomorrow." Brian heaved out a breath. "I'm sorry."

"It's all good. You're hurting. I'm an easy target." Topher

frowned down at his spaghetti. Hurting people tended to lash out. Vanessa lashed out. A lot. At least around him. What was hurting her? Maybe . . . did he owe her an apology?

He was a baker. He ought to be able to figure out a way to make crow palatable.

7

Vanessa leaned against the counter and glanced at the clock hanging on the wall in the workroom. Only another half hour and she could get out of her shoes and into thick socks and sweatpants. She'd ignore the fact that they'd topped out in the low 90s for today's high. She needed cozy. And a chick flick.

Which her brother would refuse to watch.

She sighed. There had to be some way to get him out of the house and back on his feet. Except he seemed perfectly content to hang. He did whatever she asked at the shop—so that was a bonus—but he was wasting his talent. He had an MBA and had taken several of the actuarial exams. There was so much he could do. He just had to choose it.

She'd been ducking her mom's calls since Labor Day. There was no way she was going to manage to keep Jamie's return a secret. She didn't even want to. Her parents might have a strange way of showing it, but they loved their children.

"Hey, Nessa?" Jamie poked his head into the workroom. "Can you come out front for a sec?"

"Sure. What's up?" She pushed off the counter, her feet

screaming in protest when she took a step. These shoes had to go. They'd been purchased in a moment of weakness, when her common sense was swayed by the glittery straps and sexy open toes. She might be a professional woman, but her feet were better suited to sneakers and flats.

Jamie shrugged as she passed him. "You'll see."

Great. Her customer smile faltered as her gaze landed on Topher holding a bouquet of flowers wrapped in plain white paper. Her wrapping paper had the shop name and logo printed on it, so he hadn't bought them. Which meant they'd come with him? "Kind of like bringing coals to Newcastle, isn't it?"

It took a second before he grinned. "Maybe a little. Hi."

"Hi." Vanessa peered, trying to get a better look at the blooms. It was a decent arrangement, for all it looked like one of the cheap ones men in trouble picked up at the grocery store. "Those look fresh. What'd you do?"

"What do you mean?"

"It's a classic 'sorry I goofed up' arrangement. You want to thread in a few nicer flowers to make it pop? It'll probably help her get over whatever it is you did this time." It had to be *this time*. Frankly, as abrasive as he was, she was a little amazed he didn't have a standing order with a florist somewhere.

"This ti—no. They're for you." Topher thrust the arrangement toward her.

Vanessa stepped back. "Have you hit your head?"

"Would you just take them? Sheesh."

"Fine." Vanessa reached for the flowers and lowered her head into the petals.

"Don't—" Topher stepped forward, hands up, then winced. "Smell them."

Vanessa brushed a finger across her nose and looked at the bright pink smear of frosting that came away. "They're cupcakes."

"They are." Topher dug in his pocket and produced a handkerchief. "Here."

"Thanks." She set the cupcakes down on the counter and swiped at her nose. "Did I get it?"

"Almost. Let me." He held out his hand for the cloth.

Vanessa studied him a moment before handing it back. Topher leaned across the counter. Her breath hitched. His eyes had little yellow flecks mixed in the sea of green, and there were hints of red hiding in his hair that sparkled under the shop lights.

"There. All better." His gaze met hers and she swallowed. Topher eased back and stuffed the handkerchief back into his pocket. "They taste better than they smell."

If her heart would stop racing, she might be able to catch her breath and speak. As it was, she stared at him.

He gestured to the arrangement on the counter. "The cupcakes?"

Come on, Vanessa. Heat flooded her cheeks. "I'm sure they're great. Why are they here?"

The flash of his smile didn't reach his eyes. In fact, if Vanessa was labeling it, she'd call it resigned. Which was ridiculous. Him being there was ridiculous. This whole thing was ridiculous!

"I guess I realized you and I seem to have gotten off on the wrong foot and stayed there. I thought—hoped—there might be a way to bury the hatchet." He shrugged and tucked his hands in his pockets. "You say things with flowers. I say it with cake. I thought those might split the difference."

What was his angle? "The Turner wedding. You don't want table decorations in your precious cake space, right?"

Topher's eyebrows drew together and he shook his head. "No. Whatever your plan is, I'm sure it's lovely. I've never faulted—"

"Because I've spent a lot of time on those arrangements.

They're already paid for. If you think you get to say what flowers go where, you need to seriously rethink your life. And cupcakes? Really? If you have a problem with the flowers, take it up with the bride!" Vanessa crossed her arms and glared at him.

Topher snorted. "You know what? I should've known better. I'll see you tomorrow, Ms. Fisher, just keep your stems out of my area until I'm set up."

"Don't forget your cupcake flowers."

"Keep them. Maybe if you eat one, you'll start to understand what sweet is." He pushed the door so hard the inset windows rattled.

Vanessa frowned down at the cupcakes, her gaze landing on the smeared frosting on one decorated to look like a pink hydrangea. Her favorite. Which he couldn't possibly know. How would he?

Jamie slipped up and slid his arm around her shoulders. "So. We're having cupcakes for dinner tonight?"

She glanced up at her brother's laughing eyes and drove her elbow into his gut. "You can have them. I'm making a salad."

"Interesting."

"Don't say 'interesting' in that tone. You're way off-base."

"Uh-huh."

Fuming, Vanessa turned on her heel and marched into the workroom. It was time to close. She had sweatpants, socks, and a chick flick waiting upstairs. A perfect Friday night. And if her brother smirked while he ate those cupcakes, she was going to kick him.

Topher? Interesting?

Not in this lifetime.

She pushed away the memory of his lips a breath away from hers as he wiped icing off her nose. Her pulse rocketed. Vanessa blew out a breath—that didn't mean anything. It was a normal, physical reaction to an attractive man.

Looks aside, she couldn't stand him. Even if she could, he hated her, so it was a moot point.

Wasn't it?

Vanessa fussed with the arrangements at the small table the bride and groom had requested for themselves. It was a last-minute change, something to do with squabbling parents and siblings. Why couldn't people let the couple have their day the way they wanted it? There was plenty of time to sit next to someone at dinner. Was a wedding reception that much different?

"Finished with the foyer. What's next?"

Jamie looked great in his charcoal pin striped suit. She'd unearthed it from the bottom of his duffel and sent it to the cleaners unsure if it could be salvaged. They'd worked a minor miracle. Jamie being here was a bigger one that only God could've managed.

"What?"

She blinked. "What what?"

"You were staring at me. Is the suit wrong?"

"No. You look great, which you know." She ran her hand down his arm. "I'm just really glad you're home."

He smiled, a hint of red dusting his cheeks. "Who knew my sister was such a sentimental fool?"

Vanessa snorted. "Yeah, that's me. Doofus. Can you get the cooler with the dessert table decorations and roll it over there, then find out when he's going to be ready for us?"

Jamie smirked.

"What?"

"Oh, nothing. I just find it hilarious that you haven't said anything about this guy—what's his name again?"

Vanessa ground her teeth together. "Topher."

"Right. Topher. Since he dropped by yesterday. With cupcake flowers. I mean come on, Nessa, that's a sweet gesture."

She offered a tight smile. She was doing her best to ignore Topher. As good as Jamie looked, he had nothing on Topher today. Same suit he wore to every wedding—although sometimes he donned a chef coat instead. Was it based on client request? Did people actually care what their caterer wore? Wasn't it enough that he looked presentable?

"—coming back to Earth any time soon?" Jamie's smirk broadened. "You were thinking about him, weren't you?"

"Absolutely not." Heat flooded her face.

Jamie leaned close and whispered, "You've always been a terrible liar."

"Just go find out when we can decorate the tables."

His eyebrows lifted and he snapped off a mocking salute before striding away.

Vanessa buried her face in her hands. She was losing her mind. And it was Topher's fault. That man . . . she growled and focused on the table arrangements again, but there was nothing to adjust. Nothing to fuss over.

Someone cleared his throat behind her.

Vanessa turned and her breath caught. He was too close. Topher was always too close. "Yes?"

"Ms. Fisher, the dessert tables await your magical touch."

She pressed her lips together. Was he making fun? It was hard to tell—the words were snide, but his tone was more like a butler informing his employer of a visitor. If she worked at it, she could replace the image of Topher with that of her parents' butler, Ralph. He and Estelle had been surrogate parents for most of her formative years, stepping in to offer unconditional love when she'd failed—again—to meet her parents' expectations.

Which happened a lot.

"Thank you." There was her mother's voice coming right out of her mouth. But it was too late.

Topher gave a short nod and walked away.

Just like he had last night.

What was wrong with her? They weren't friends. They'd never been friends. He barely tolerated her. Then, out of the blue, he showed up with cupcakes and some yarn about starting over? She snorted. Right.

Vanessa just needed to figure out what his angle was. He had one.

Everybody did.

She needed to pull it together. There were flowers to arrange for this reception. Once that was done she could head home. At least then she'd be away from whatever craziness Topher had in mind.

"You okay?" Jamie set a small arrangement of mixed yellow flowers at her elbow.

"Of course." Vanessa frowned at the flowers. "What are those doing here? They're meant to be for the ladies' luncheon tomorrow afternoon."

"They were in the cooler." Jamie shrugged. "I'll put them back in."

"Sure. Fine. Do that." But Vanessa straightened and glanced back over the reception area. Had other wrong flowers worked their way in? The color scheme was similar, but that's where it ended. The ladies' lunch flowers were inexpensive—she didn't want to call them cheap, even in her head—as she was doing the event as a favor to a friend of her mom's and not charging enough to even cover all her costs. Nothing popped out at her, but she'd do another run-through before they left.

"Problem?"

Topher was at her elbow again, leaning in. Too close. What

was with him? Vanessa huffed out a breath. "No. Don't you have . . . I don't know, something to frost?"

His laugh rolled out like thunder. "Actually, I don't. I do all the frosting at the shop. Did you enjoy your cupcakes?"

"You say that like you think I ate them all already." She hadn't even eaten a whole one. Maybe she'd nibbled the edge of one, just to see if they were edible, but that hardly counted. "Jamie said they were delicious."

It couldn't have been hurt that flashed across his face, could it? It was gone too quickly to be sure and replaced with Topher's usual mocking grin. "Don't want to ruin your figure, I guess. Your loss."

"Did you need something? I'd like to finish dressing this table and go." She carefully spread flower petals around the base of the cake plate. The effect looked effortless. It was anything but. The bride, at least, had known her colors. The natural petals matched the cake so well it was hard to tell which were real and which decoration. "You did a good job on these flowers."

One corner of Topher's mouth quirked up. "Was that a compliment?"

She spun and crossed her arms. "What is your problem?"

He held up his hands and took a step back. "No problem. Just don't want to misconstrue anything."

"Can't you just say thank you like a normal person?" And then go away. Far, far away.

"Thank you." He sighed and tucked his hands in his pockets. "You should try to eat the cupcakes before Monday or they'll get stale. Baked goods aren't as resilient as flowers. If you can't, just toss 'em. They won't be worth your time after tomorrow."

"Out of curiosity, did you honestly expect me to eat six cupcakes in three days all by myself?"

He shrugged. "It's cake. Who doesn't like cake?"

She studied him for a moment before nodding. "Did I say thank you?"

His eyes lit with laughter. "I don't seem to recall that, no."

"Then thank you. I'll be sure to eat one this afternoon. It was an interesting gesture."

His smile mocked her. "I'll let you get back to work. You've done a nice job here with the flowers."

"Thanks." She needn't have bothered saying it. He was gone before she got it out. Vanessa frowned after him.

"It's a nice view." One of the servers who often worked with Topher when he catered an event waggled her eyebrows as she paused and followed Vanessa's gaze. "Never really seen anyone fill out a suit or a chef coat like Topher. I bet he's just as hot in jeans and a t-shirt. He won't fraternize, which is a shame. Course, you don't work for him, so you might have a better shot."

"Oh. I'm not—" Heat flooded Vanessa's face. "It's not like that. At all."

"You keep telling yourself that." The girl winked. "Oh. You might want to check the flowers on table sixteen. They're not quite the same as the others."

"Sixteen. Thanks." She glanced around. Where had Jamie gone? He had a bad habit of disappearing whenever Topher showed up, leaving her to fend for herself. He'd teased her, off and on, for the bulk of the night last night. No matter how much she insisted he was off-base. Men.

She turned her attention back to the dessert table and finished setting out the flowers. If she snuck a peek over her shoulder, it was because she was trying to find her brother. She wasn't looking for Topher.

She wasn't looking for Topher at all.

8

Topher stretched his legs out in front of him and breathed deep. At peace, he watched the water flowing out of the mouth of the fish standing on its tail in the center of the sunken garden at Peacock Hill. "This is nice."

"Right?" Jeremiah Crawford tossed a pebble into the pool at the base of the fountain and let out a noisy sigh. "Duncan outdid himself getting the gardens back together."

"Where is he? And Sean? Isn't Sean supposed to be here?" Sean had extended the invitation to meet for lunch and hanging out at Peacock Hill. Topher had assumed that meant his friend would be here as well. He knew the gang here passably, but not so well he would just show up uninvited.

Jeremiah shrugged. "They'll be along, I imagine. Matt, too."

"Aren't he and—oh, his wife, what's her name? Cyan? Skye?"

"Ha. No, she's Azure. Her brother is Cyan. And I think her sister is Skye, if you can believe it. And yes, they're just back from their honeymoon, if that's what you were going to ask." Jeremiah sifted a handful of gravel through his fingers. "But Deidre and Claire convinced her to go to Charlottesville for a baby registry. So. Matt's at loose ends. Or so he says."

"So he does." Matt skipped down the steps into the garden and flopped onto one of the benches along the perimeter. "But if I'd known it was going to be a garden party, I might have waved off. There's a lot of work to do at the house. And the garage."

"What's wrong with the house?" Jeremiah stood and dusted the back of his shorts. "I had cleaners in and everything."

Matt glanced at Topher. "You're the cake guy—Chris?"

"The other half of the name—Topher. That's me. If Sean isn't going to—"

"Don't be stupid, man. Hang. You were at the house that one time, right? This summer? Nachos."

Topher nodded at Matt and settled back.

"So you know Azure and I bought Jeremiah's old place now that he's here?"

"I guess I kind of remember something about that." Topher shrugged. It didn't matter to him, but it was nice to get caught up. "Baby registry?"

Jeremiah grinned. "Yeah. Deidre's due in early February, but her mom's already pushing for a baby shower now that we're out of the first trimester."

"Aren't you supposed to wait until then to tell people?" Topher pursed his lips. He'd heard something like that somewhere, hadn't he? "I have no personal pregnancy experience, obviously, but I thought that was a thing."

"Don't look at me." Matt shrugged. "We're not planning to need to know that for a while yet. Not that there's anything wrong with diving in right off."

Jeremiah chuckled. "Wasn't exactly what we'd planned on either, but you roll with what comes. It's going to be fun."

"You thought about how it's going to work with your apartment downstairs though? It's a great space for a couple. Maybe even one kid. But more than that?" Matt shook his head.

"We're talking about moving the business center to one of

the main floor rooms. It's not used very often, to be honest, so it's not as if we couldn't tuck a computer and printer into the breakfast room and call it done. And," Jeremiah glanced around before lowering his voice, "I've overheard Claire on a couple of phone calls lately and am starting to worry that she's thinking of moving back north. But you can't say anything to anyone. I could be wrong."

Matt winced. "That'll destroy Deidre."

Jeremiah nodded.

Topher struggled to keep up. He knew the players, but mostly didn't understand what the big deal was. "Claire is Deidre's sister?"

Jeremiah nodded. "You can't possibly be interested, sorry. Sean and Duncan should be here soon. I think Danny's actually going to come, too. Once they get here, we can head to the bonfire clearing. I set up some targets."

"Targets?" Topher swallowed. He was more of a frost the cake and then hit up the game console kind of guy. Guns were not his thing.

"Archery, man. Bow hunting starts in three weeks."

"Bow hunting. Like shooting animals on purpose?" Topher's insides constricted. "That's pretty far outside my wheelhouse."

Matt laughed. "For today it's just paper. We won't make you shoot a deer if you don't want to."

"Who's shooting deer?" Sean jogged down into the garden. "Sorry I'm late. Brides. And whoever isn't shooting deer—I'm hanging out with them."

Topher grinned. "I knew there was a reason we were friends."

Jeremiah shook his head. "Seriously? You don't know what you're missing."

Danny and Duncan arrived together.

Duncan shot Danny a glare before crossing to peer into the fountain and scoop out a couple of rocks. "Who's missing what?"

"Neither of the city boys want to go bow hunting." Jeremiah shook his head. "Imagine that means you also don't want venison?"

Topher made a face. "I'll pass."

Sean jerked a thumb toward Topher. "Still with him."

Danny snickered. "Are you two ladies even willing to aim at paper targets?"

"You sure you have permission from what's her name to be here, Danny?" Duncan's voice dripped with scorn. "She give you your pants for the night?"

"What is your problem? Casey's cool. Which you'd all know if you'd hang out with her for more than two minutes at a time." Danny's hands bunched into fists. "Maybe I should just head home, since it's obvious no one wants me here."

Matt scowled at Duncan before standing. "Stay. Duncan's going to stop ragging on you, and you're going to stop rubbing your girlfriend in his sister's face."

"In his—Claire? Like she cares. You're way off-base there, man."

Topher shook his head. Some people only saw what they wanted to see. He hadn't been around the gang a lot, but even he could tell Claire had a thing for the guy. Granted, he'd been let in on the secret—could it be called a secret when nearly everyone knew?—but once they said something, it had been obvious.

"Why don't we head up to the clearing?" Matt started up the steps on the far side of the sunken garden.

Topher hung back and fell into step beside Sean. "Did you know this was going to be a hunting thing?"

"Nope. Just got the invite and they said to feel free to bring you." Sean shrugged. "You kind of have to figure guys who grow up rural like this are going to be into that, don't you?"

"I guess. Ever shot a bow?"

Sean laughed. "I think it was a unit in P.E. in the ninth grade. I don't remember much beyond not pointing the arrow at other people, even if you were playing around."

"Sounds about right. How's Larissa?"

"She said she was spending the afternoon with the cat grading papers."

"She's enjoying teaching then?"

"Very much."

"You planning on getting her a ring?"

Sean tripped over a tree root and frowned. "Where'd that come from?"

Topher chuckled. "Last week at church."

"Speaking of church—didn't see you there this morning."

He'd thought about it. A lot. "I wasn't sure that was such a good idea. There are a lot of options in Richmond."

"You try any of them?"

"No, Mom, not this week."

Sean grinned. "Touchy. So you didn't like it?"

"No, I did. I—" Topher broke off and sighed. "I didn't want to run into Vanessa again. After our conversation last week and then a talk with Brian, I went over to her shop Friday night with some cupcakes. Sort of a peace offering."

"Yeah? How'd that go?"

"She didn't throw them at me, but it wasn't much better. Then yesterday—"

"Wait. Yesterday?"

"Wedding at a local country club. Vanessa was there and it was just weird. I don't know what I'm doing."

Sean nodded. "Sorry, man. This couple . . . had they been together like five years? With a kid?"

"That's them."

"Ah. Yeah, they didn't like my attitude."

Topher laughed. "I admire your stance, man, but I don't know how you do it."

"I guess it's a matter of trying to live out what I feel God is saying to me, you know? I'm not going to tell you not to make cakes for people, though. You're praying over your business, you'll follow God's lead."

Topher slowed as they entered the clearing and took note of the hay bales set up on the far side. Targets were fixed to the fronts and several bows rested against the logs arranged around the fire pit. The other guys were already picking up the equipment and checking it out. He glanced at Sean. "Brian really respects you for it, if that helps."

"Yeah? How're their plans going?"

"Pretty sure that's done, actually. Brian's been crashing at my place."

"That's rough."

Topher nodded and watched as Matt notched an arrow in place, pulled back, and let it soar. It struck dead center of the target. "We're going to get our hats handed to us, aren't we?"

Sean blew out a breath. "Looks like it."

Topher's stomach was growling and his arm stung as he dropped onto one of the logs. "I'm done."

"Me, too." Sean took a seat beside Topher. "It's harder than it looks."

"Tell me." Topher held out his left arm. The skin was dark red along the inside of his forearm. "How bad a bruise do you think that's going to make?"

"I told you to roll your arm." Jeremiah grabbed Topher's

wrist and frowned. "Sorry, man. Next time I'll look around harder for the arm and finger guards."

"Uh-huh. Next time, maybe you can all come to my bakery and I'll let you make cakes and conveniently forget where I put the pot holders when it comes time to get them out of the oven."

Sean snickered.

Jeremiah laughed. "It's probably fair. Would nachos make up for it?"

"Aw man, not nachos. It's always nachos." Danny made a gagging motion. "While I'll concede you're the nacho king, couldn't we grill burgers or something for once?"

"I have to second that." Matt raised his hand with a half shrug. "Sorry."

"Wow. I see how it is." Jeremiah's smile belied any insult. "Let me text Deidre and see if we have anything with which to make said burgers. If not, we could head into town and grab a bite at the diner."

Topher checked the time on his phone. "I—maybe I should head back. My days start early on Monday and there's still stuff I need to do."

"You still have to eat. Leave after dinner. Let's just head into town. I haven't hit the diner in a while. We haven't grilled you about your love life either. You're the only one left." Danny's grin was sharp.

"That'll be a short conversation." Topher stood. "But I like burgers, and I'd rather not drive home starving or hit fast food on the way."

"Can I hook a ride with you?" Sean pushed to his feet.

"Yeah, okay." Topher glanced at Jeremiah. "Town's not big— am I going to miss the diner?"

"Not unless you've got your eyes closed. Whoever gets there first, ask for the big table in the back corner." Jeremiah slipped his leg through one of the bows and leaned backward, working at the top for a moment until the string loosened. "I've got to stow the equipment, so it'll be a few."

"I can help with that." Matt grabbed one of the bows and unstrung it.

Danny sighed. "Yeah, me too. You two go ahead."

"Guess that puts me on arrow collection." Duncan strode off toward the hay bales.

"We can—"

Jeremiah cut Topher off with a shake of his head. "Go on down. We won't be far behind you."

With a shrug, Sean started toward the front of the house.

Topher jogged until he caught up. "Did that seem a little more strained than usual?"

"If by a little you mean a lot? Yeah. It did. I'm guessing Danny and this Casey person are part of it. The guys are protective of Claire. I don't get the feeling Danny's ever looked in her direction seriously."

"That stinks. It's not fun to realize you've got feelings for someone who has no interest in you. Or, maybe worse even, despises you."

"Hmm. Thus speaks the voice of experience?" Sean jabbed Topher in the side with his elbow. "You're holding out. Who're you hung up on?"

What was it about Sean at Peacock Hill? Topher always ended up saying too much when he was here. "Nobody."

"Bzzt. Not buying it. Not after that comment. Come on, spill. Who am I going to tell?"

Topher clicked the unlock button on his fob and frowned at Sean. "Oh, I don't know, your fiancée?"

"Nice try." Sean slid into the passenger seat and reached for his seatbelt. "Okay, fine. I'll admit I've been perusing a few online diamond retailers. Now you 'fess up."

"Listen to you, 'online diamond retailers'." Topher snorted. "What's wrong with the jewelry stores in town?"

"Too many people who know me. I go in one of them and buy a ring? Larissa is going to know about it before I finish signing the receipt."

Topher considered as he navigated the driveway down to the windy country road that led down into town. "More than likely. Richmond might be a city, but there's a lot of small town in there, too."

"Exactly."

"You can see why maybe I don't want my own issue getting out? I'll probably come to my senses soon anyway. We'd be horrible together. I think I'm just projecting some subconscious desire for a relationship onto the only seriously available person I know, even though I also know she's completely wrong for me."

Sean sent Topher a bland stare. "You keeping daytime TV on at the bakery?"

Topher laughed and ran a hand over his face. "I do sound like a talk show, don't I? It's Vanessa. I can't stop thinking about Vanessa."

"I. Wow. That's unexpected. You loathe her."

"Right?"

"So the cupcakes?"

Topher groaned. "The cupcakes prove that I need to figure out a way to get over myself. As did our interactions at the event yesterday."

"No. No, slow down there. I . . . can kind of see the two of you working. If I squint really hard."

"Just don't. I'm going to come to my senses very soon now. I can feel it." Maybe if he kept saying that, it'd happen. Or he'd at least stop losing time wondering what it'd be like to feel her lips on his. Didn't curiosity kill the cat or something? "Is that the diner?"

Sean glanced out the window. "Looks like."

"Can you not mention this conversation? Ever?"

Sean laughed. "All right. But if you want someone to talk to, you know where to find me. I have some experience with challenging relationships."

Topher nodded and aimed for an open street parking spot just down from the diner. He didn't want to talk to anyone about his feelings for Vanessa. He didn't want to *have* feelings for Vanessa.

She was exactly the kind of complication he didn't need in his life right now.

9

Vanessa rolled her head on her neck. She'd spent her day on arrangements for a baby shower being held tomorrow afternoon. The grandma-to-be was due to pick them up any minute and then? Then she was going to close. It might be thirty minutes early, but she didn't care.

The phone rang at the same time as the door chime.

Because nothing was ever easy.

"Jamie? Grab the phone, will you?" She wasn't completely sure he heard her. He'd disappeared into the storeroom fifteen minutes or so ago and she hadn't seen him since. For all she knew, he'd stretched out for a nap. But the phone cut off, so maybe that was a good sign.

Fixing a smile on her face, she stepped into the storefront and froze, her brain scrambling to catch up. "Mom."

Her mother held open her arms with a smile. "Hello, darling."

Vanessa slid around the counter and stepped into her hug. She brushed her lips across her mom's cheek before scooting back. "What brings you all this way?"

"I can't want to see my daughter's shop? And my daughter?"

Since that hadn't enticed her mom out this direction in the three years she'd been in business, it seemed unlikely, but she knew better than to say anything. "Of course. And it's a lovely surprise. I was just thinking I might close early—as soon as the flowers for an event tomorrow are picked up."

"Hey Nessa, that was . . ." Jamie came in through the doorway, phone in his hand. He stopped, glanced back the way he'd just come, then set the phone on the counter. "Mrs. Larsen. She's going to come tomorrow morning first thing instead. There's a complication with the caterer that she's caught up with tonight. Hi, Mom."

"James?" Her mother's eyes filled and her arms dropped to her side. "You're here? All this time?"

"No. I just got here."

"Two weeks. Ish." Vanessa cleared her throat. "He was here when I got home from the Labor Day cookout."

"You didn't call. Either of you. Why wouldn't you call?" She wrapped her arms around herself and stared up at the ceiling.

Vanessa glared at her brother. Why hadn't she insisted? She'd mentioned contacting their parents a few times, but had never pushed. Now she was just as much to blame as he was.

Jamie's shoulders fell and he crossed to their mom, wrapping her stiff form in his arms. "I didn't know how. I wouldn't let Nessa. This isn't on her."

"I wish you wouldn't call her that. She's not some imaginary lake monster."

Jamie's grin flashed as he stepped back and tucked his hands in his pockets. "She is to me."

"We should celebrate. Since I don't have a pickup tonight after all, let's close now and go grab some dinner." Vanessa started toward the door. She caught sight of her mother's car idling at the curb and fought the urge to roll her eyes. "Let me get Ralph to pull around the back. There's a nice little place a couple of blocks away. We can walk."

"No."

Vanessa turned when her mother spoke, her brow furrowing. "What?"

"I said no. Your father's not here. When we celebrate your brother's return, he should be here. Friday. At home. I'll expect the two of you by five so you can be settled before the guests arrive."

"Guests? Mom, that's not—I'm not—it's—"

"James. It's exactly what should be done when your father's son and heir returns from his time abroad. I'll keep the party small." She eyed him, her lips thinning. "Be sure to deal with your hair before then. You can both stay the weekend."

"Mom, I can't—"

This time she cut off Vanessa. "You can and will. Your brother is home. It's time for family. I'm sure there are people you use when conflicts arise. Find them."

The door jangled as Topher pushed it open, a white bakery box in his hands. "Hey—oh, sorry. You've got a client, I can wait."

Vanessa closed her eyes and tried to imagine this was a dream. She pushed her lips into her brightest smile. "Topher, this is my mother. Mom, meet my . . ." What? He wasn't a friend, exactly. Co-worker? Not really. Acquaintance? That would probably annoy him. "Topher. He's a baker."

"Your Topher?" Her mother's eyes lit with interest as she turned and extended her hand. "It's a pleasure to meet you. I'd like to say we've heard a lot about you, but I believe Vanessa's been keeping a lot of secrets these days. Are you free on Friday?"

"Yes, ma'am."

"Good. You'll come along for the welcome home dinner for James. We'll keep it casual. A suit and tie will be fine."

"Mom . . ." Vanessa dug around for words.

"That sounds lovely. Thank you." Topher smiled.

Vanessa ground her teeth.

"Great." Vanessa's mother beamed at both her children. "I'll call with details when I get home tonight. After I've had a chance to chat with your father. He's going to be so pleased."

All Vanessa could do was nod.

Jamie didn't even manage that much.

Topher lifted a hand in a wave.

When her mother had climbed into the back seat of her car, Vanessa turned to Topher. "What was that?"

"Well now. If I'm 'your Topher,' I didn't see how I could say no." Laughter glittered in his eyes.

Vanessa buried her face in her hands and fought the urge to scream.

Jamie snickered. "He has a point."

"Got you off the hook." Topher slapped Jamie's back.

"That you did. Thanks, man."

"Glad to help. I was just dropping by with another treat."

Vanessa blew out a breath. "I thought I explained I don't really eat sweets."

"Open the box, why don't you, before you jump down my throat."

"I wasn't—" Okay, she was. She took a deep breath. Then another. What was it about Topher that circumvented her ability to keep a hold on her temper? She reached for the box and flipped open the lid. Strawberries glistened on a thin puff of flaky pastry. Her mouth watered. She looked up and met Topher's gaze.

"Well?"

"Thank you. They look amazing."

"Was that so hard?"

Harder than it should have been.

"I guess you'll be in touch about Friday. Do you have my number?"

"I can call the bakery."

Topher shook his head and pulled out his phone. He tapped at the screen a moment and her cell chimed. "There. Since I never did text you to let you know you could come decorate the cake tent at the Labor Day wedding."

She didn't want his contact information in there. But she also couldn't text the bakery. Texting was better than actually talking to him. Much better. "Great. Thanks."

If he caught the dripping sarcasm, Topher didn't let on. "Were you busy for dinner tonight?"

Jamie leaned on the counter with a grin. "She mentioned someplace close—walking distance—to Mom. I'm always up for a meal I don't have to cook."

"You don't cook upstairs."

"Not true. I made pancakes."

A shriek wedged in her throat and she forced her words out around it, only imagining pulling on her hair instead of doing it in reality. "One time. A week and a half ago."

"Sounds like a night out is just what you need then." Topher jerked his head toward the door. "Why don't you lock up and we'll go? My treat."

A hundred different responses warred in her mind as Vanessa stared at him. Finally, she choked out, "Why?"

"Because I'm hungry and a walk sounds good. You don't want to come, I won't take it personally." Topher tucked his hands in his pockets.

Vanessa took a deep breath and reached for the bakery box. "I need a couple minutes to run these upstairs. Jamie, you'll lock up?"

Jamie nodded.

"Great. I'll meet you out front in a few." Clutching her fruit tarts, Vanessa hurried out the back door. How was this happening? Topher had neatly boxed her in, that's how. Both with dinner tonight and the one at home on Friday.

At the top of the stairs, she rested her head against the front door. Ambushed from all sides. And Friday? Dread curled in her stomach. That had been a true no-win. Maybe Topher's decision was the better of them. It wasn't as if she had anything planned. The less she made of it, the less her mother would. So Topher would come to dinner and then that would be that. She wouldn't owe him. He could've said no. She definitely didn't owe him anything.

Wouldn't.

Didn't.

"I LIKE HIM." Jamie stretched out his legs and propped his feet on the coffee table before taking an enormous bite of one of the fruit tarts Topher had delivered that evening.

"You would." Vanessa scowled at the tart before using a knife to cut off a small, bite-sized square from the corner. Whatever else she had to say about him, Topher could bake. There was enough sweetness for this to be a dessert, but it wasn't overpowering or cloying.

"Come on, dinner was fun. He seems like a nice guy. What's your deal?" Jamie demolished the rest of his pastry in three fast bites.

Vanessa frowned and sliced off another tiny bite. "How do you eat like that and stay thin? It's completely unfair."

Jamie grinned and pointed a finger at her. "Good genes. Same ones you have, but you don't choose to test out. Don't try to change the subject."

"He's just so smug and irritating. And he's always in my way."

Jamie snickered. "Topher? The guy we went to dinner with? The one who held your chair out for you and kept turning the conversation back to you—or to me—and hardly said two words about his own life?"

"Did I ask him to hold my chair? I've been sitting down for close to thirty years now. I know how it works."

"Nessa."

"What?" She took a deep breath and stared at the tart before pushing it away.

"It's obvious he likes you. You should cut him some slack." Jamie nodded at her tart. "Are you going to eat that?"

"You can have it." Topher didn't like her. Not in any definition of the word. He had to find her every bit as irritating as she did him. "You've seen him at weddings—how he treats me?"

Jamie strolled to the table and dragged her plate closer. He plucked a berry off the top and popped it in his mouth. "Granted I've only done one event with you that he was at, but you're not making your case here. He was deferential and polite. So it circles back around to what's your deal?"

Was this really all her problem? No. "Look. Maybe I can give you the fact that he seems a little different now. But we've worked together off and on for going on maybe three years, and he has never been this pleasant to me. Ever."

"So you don't trust it."

"Would you?"

Jamie frowned and looked away, his lips pressed together. "People change. Sometimes for good. Sometimes not. Sometimes they go one way and then they come back around the other."

Vanessa reached out and covered her brother's hand.

"You forgave me—welcomed me home—all without any proof that I'd changed or had any desire to. Mom, in her way, did the same. I imagine Dad will, too."

"You're my brother, Jamie."

The corners of his mouth lifted. "Sure, but Jesus didn't limit that kind of grace and love to family members."

She winced.

He flipped his hand over and squeezed her fingers. "Seems to me he's probably not the only one who's changed. And he's making an effort. So maybe . . ."

Vanessa sighed. "Maybe I need to make an effort too."

Jamie nodded and shoveled the rest of her tart into his mouth. "Plus, he makes superior baked goods. That's a friend—or more—worth having."

"Let's try to work our way up to friend before we worry about the 'or more' part, okay?" Vanessa glanced at her phone when it rang. "There's Mom."

"You get that. I'm going to go for a walk."

"You're coming back though, right?"

Jamie bent down and kissed her cheek. "I'm coming back. I'm done running."

That was something, at least. Vanessa pushed thoughts of Topher and people changing to the back of her mind and fixed on a bright smile as she answered the call, "Hi, Mom."

10

"Snazzy." Brian crossed his arms and leaned against the kitchen counter. "Hot date?"

Topher adjusted the knot on his tie. "Sort of. But not really."

"Stop fiddling with that tie. You just messed it up." Brian drummed his fingers on his arm. "This is that dinner with the flower girl's parents. It's barely one in the afternoon. Why are you already in a suit?"

"Because apparently said parents live in Winchester, of all places. So there's a bit of a drive involved."

Brian whistled. "Horse money out there."

"All kinds of money out there. Having seen Vanessa's mother, I'm guessing I'll get to rub elbows with some of it at dinner tonight. The woman screams posh and polish."

"You sound surprised."

Topher shrugged. "Vanessa doesn't have the same vibe. She gives off the pretty standard suburban upbringing thing. You know?"

"So maybe it's new money? Since Vanessa left home."

"Could be. I don't figure I'm going to find out. If Vanessa's family hasn't come up in the three-ish years I've known her, I don't see her excited to start now."

Brian nodded. "Points for her, though. None of that 'my daddy this' bit all the time."

That was a reasonable point. One he'd have to factor in, because most of the time when he started thinking too much about how much money she must come from, Topher started getting annoyed. Her prices had cost her a handful of jobs that he knew about. And sure, there was nothing wrong with setting out to be on the higher end of wedding services, but were her costs really that much more than other florists? She didn't have staff. Overhead on the building was probably high. Except now that he knew about the family money, maybe mommy and daddy had bought it for her.

"What's going on in that brain of yours? You like the woman —that much is obvious. And you maneuvered yourself into this date. So why are you acting like you're not sure now?"

"I don't know." Topher ran a hand through his hair. "Honestly? I was playing around when I agreed to this. I figured Vanessa would nip it in the bud and tear a strip off me to boot. She's never been shy about making her opinion on everything known. I don't get why she suddenly agreed to let me come."

"I guess you'll have to figure that out." Brian frowned. "What are you taking her?"

"Taking her? Why would I take her something?"

"You're picking up a date. That means you take the woman some flowers."

"She's a florist. I'm not taking her flowers."

Brian waved away the objection. "Fine. Not flowers. Something. Cookies? Cake pops?"

"She makes a point of saying how she doesn't eat sweets. I have a torte for her parents—hostess gift. Why do I need more than that?" Topher strode to the fridge and removed the box holding the torte. It was good Brian had reminded him about that, at least. He'd nearly left without it. Vanessa's mom didn't seem like the kind of woman who'd let a social slight like that go without a few digs. Or, at least, not without adding a couple of chalk marks in the negative column when it came to approving him as worthy of her daughter.

Which shouldn't matter.

But it did.

"Trust me on this one. That woman needs a gift. Even if it's a single flower. She's a florist, so you know she likes blooms. Get her one." Brian shook his head. "How is it that I know more about wooing a woman than you do?"

Topher laughed. "There's a question. All right. I'll defer to your expertise and swing by the grocery store and grab something."

Brian winced. "That'll do, I guess. Just don't let her know where you got it, okay? She'll be appalled."

"Got it. Anything else?"

"Nope. But I expect a full report when you get back. Since I have no romantic possibilities on my radar right now, I'm going to live vicariously through yours. Don't let me down."

Topher shook his head. He'd overheard Brian on the phone with Dave a couple of times. There hadn't been shouting, so he'd assumed the two of them might be trying to work things out. He should ask—except he didn't really want details. And Brian was big on details. What Topher wanted, what he prayed for constantly, was for Brian to find Jesus. Brian was big on asking Topher to pray for him to be happy. There was nothing wrong with happiness.

But Jesus could give his friend joy.

Topher would much rather pray for that.

～

TOPHER LET out a low whistle as they turned into the circular drive in front of Vanessa's parents' house. "Some place. What's your dad do again?"

"He's semi-retired."

Uh-huh. That was now. He wasn't going to push. He'd meet the man himself in a few minutes anyway, and it'd probably come up in conversation. It always seemed to. Right before they tacked on "how interesting" to the reminder that he was a baker. Because respectable men didn't become bakers? He was never sure what the issue was.

"So you didn't grow up here?"

Vanessa sighed. "No. I did."

He nodded. Her tone effectively ended that conversation. And up until now, they'd actually been getting along well. That had, in fact, been a relief. There wasn't much worse than a three hour drive filled with awkward silence. At least that had held off until they'd arrived. Topher cleared his throat. "Should I park anywhere special?"

She pointed. "Just there past the main stairs. That's where I always leave my car. If they need it moved, they'll send someone in to get the keys."

"Okay. And Jamie—James?—is meeting us here? I'd half expected to give him a ride, too." Not that he was complaining about having some extra time with Vanessa on his own. He could pretend they were on a date.

Wait. What?

Not a date. Neither of them expected this to be a date. If anything, it was a chance to get to know what made her tick. Spend some time away from the pressure cooker of a wedding.

Maybe see if a date could be in their future.

Topher glanced over at her as he parked.

"He came down on Wednesday. After Mom stopped by, he figured he might as well get a head start on groveling."

"Ah. Think it would really be that bad?" Just what sort of family gathering was he getting himself into? Not that Vanessa's mom had given him much of a choice. And he'd been too intrigued to decline more forcibly.

"No. I've been trying—subtly, mind you—to get him to go home since he showed up on my doorstep. Literally. Mom showing up clinched it. Not that he'll necessarily stay here. In fact, if he's smart, he'll choose another town in Virginia. Something a couple of hours away."

"Like you did?" Topher pushed open his car door and hurried around to Vanessa's side, but she was already stepping out. He opened the back door and carefully lifted the bakery box from the floor.

"Just like I did. I love my parents. Being three hours away makes it easier."

Topher laughed. "That I understand. My folks moved to Florida when they retired. It has made it a lot easier to overlook the times when I feel like they're meddling or criticizing, and they're convinced they're looking after my best interests."

Vanessa nodded and pressed the doorbell. Chimes echoed from behind the door and Topher grinned. "Westminster. They're a classic for a reason."

"Mom says they're dignified." Vanessa smiled as the door opened. She stepped forward and enveloped the uniformed woman in a hug. "Hi, Estelle. How is it?"

"Miss Vanessa. Twice in a month is a good surprise. Your father's beside himself with joy now your brother's home. Your mother, too, in her way."

"That's about what I figured. Dad trying to get Jamie to step in and take over so he can fully retire?"

"You know he is." Estelle met Topher's gaze then looked at Vanessa. "Now I understand you've been keeping secrets from your mother. I can't say I blame you on that front, but I would've thought you'd tell me. Introduce me to your young man."

Vanessa's cheeks pinked. "Oh, he's not—"

Topher shifted the torte to his left arm and extended his hand. "Topher Adams. It's a pleasure to meet you."

"So polite. That'll go over well with your father." Estelle took Topher's hand with a wink. "I'm Estelle. I keep the house."

"Please. She's family." When Estelle opened her mouth, Vanessa shook her head. "Don't bother. Everyone knows it. Where are they?"

"The sunroom." Estelle smiled. "You might try to enjoy yourself. Your parents are in a good mood. So is James. Don't be the one who drags a black cloud into the room."

"Right." Vanessa glanced at Topher. "You ready for this?"

He gave a half-shrug. "I don't see why not."

He wasn't one hundred percent positive, but it sounded like Vanessa muttered, "You will." Then she took his hand and gave a gentle tug. "This way. Thanks, Estelle."

"I like your house." Topher ignored the fact that she was still clinging to his hand. Or he tried to ignore it, at least. That had to count for something.

"Thanks. Look, I'm still not sure why you let yourself get signed up for this, but I appreciate it."

He grinned. "That wasn't so hard, was it?"

"Vanessa, you made it." Her mother stood and crossed the room. She wrapped Vanessa in a hug and beamed at Topher. "And —Topher, wasn't it? I'm so glad you could come, too, so we can all get acquainted. Come in and sit. What can we get you to drink?"

Topher held out the bakery box as he scanned the glasses already on the table. "I brought this for you. Is that iced tea?"

"Oh. Thank you. It is. No one makes sweet tea like Estelle. Vanessa?"

"Sure. Sounds good. Thanks, Mom."

Vanessa's mother took the bakery box and waved a hand at her daughter. "Introduce Topher to your father, dear, while I get the drinks."

Vanessa tugged his hand some more as she entered the room and circled the table to where a bear of a man sat talking to James. "Daddy, this is Topher Adams."

The man stopped mid-word and stood, extending his hand. "Topher, nice to meet you. Call me James."

Topher's gaze flicked to Vanessa's brother before he grasped the man's hand. "It's a pleasure to meet you, Sir."

James boomed out a laugh. "Have a seat. I believe I understand you already know my son?"

"We've met a couple of times, yes. Good to see you again."

Jamie shook his head and kicked out the chair beside him. "What'd you bring?"

Topher held the chair for Vanessa, then took the one beside her. He didn't need to be right next to her family. "Why don't we wait for your mother to open it? She might not want to get into it yet."

"Can't blame a guy for trying. Especially not when I know how good your treats are. Even Nessa enjoyed those fruit things, and she doesn't usually bother with desserts."

What was the point in life without dessert? Okay, maybe Topher could see giving up sweets if there were medical conditions in play, but without that? A treat now and then made every day a little brighter. But to each their own. He winked at Vanessa. "I'm glad you liked them."

Vanessa jammed her elbow into her brother's side. "I'm not that bad. I just don't make a habit of having nothing but sugar for any of the major meals. You may have the metabolism of a teenager still, but I'm pushing thirty and can tell."

"Well, the rest of us can't." Topher reached for the glass of iced tea Vanessa's mother held out. "Thank you."

"That torte is beautiful."

"Thank you, again." Topher smiled. "It should last in the fridge for two or three days if you want to wait to eat it."

"Oh, no, I thought we could put it out this evening with the rest of the desserts. Is that all right?" Vanessa's mom slid into a chair next to her husband.

"Of course. I appreciate the invitation this evening. Welcoming Jamie—James—home is a family matter."

"Well, family and close friends. Several of our closest friends will be joining us for supper. They've been faithful in praying for James' return. It would·be unthinkable to exclude them from celebrating his homecoming."

Jamie shifted in his seat, looking mortified. "Mom. I still don't think—"

She held up her hand. "James. We've had this conversation."

Vanessa's father chuckled and patted Jamie on the shoulder. "Better all around if you let it go. She's arranged the party. What else are we supposed to do when the prodigal returns? Now, Topher—is that short for Christopher?"

"Normally it would be, but my parents have always been a little non-traditional, so they just named me Topher. They didn't want people deciding to call me Chris instead." Topher shrugged. "It's never bothered me. Even with the strange looks I sometimes get when I'm signing official documents."

"Good for you. I'm afraid we saddled James as a junior."

"Not junior, the second," Vanessa's mom interjected.

Humor sparked in the older man's eyes. "As you can see, it's been a point of dissension since."

The peal of the Westminster Chimes cut off further conversation. Vanessa's parents exchanged a glance before her mom rose. "I'll go help Estelle greet the guests. James, honey, why don't you and the children go out onto the patio and make sure everything's set?"

Vanessa leaned over and whispered in Topher's ear, "Everything's been set for at least two hours, if I know my mother."

Topher reached for her hand and gave it a light squeeze. The mix of nerves and embarrassment was a new look for Vanessa, and he struggled to understand it. Her parents seemed nice enough. There'd been no hidden barbs in their words. Sure, they were a little snooty. A little awkward—as if they were trying to be funny and warm and were out of practice.

Vanessa flipped her hand over and laced her fingers through Topher's, clinging like he was a lifeline.

He barely managed to keep his reaction neutral as her father's gaze zeroed in on their linked hands.

The older man stood, clapped Jamie on the shoulder, and gestured to the french doors leading to a lush outside space. "Shall we? I'll make sure the music's playing and the space heaters are ready to turn on if it starts to get chilly. Everything else is ready, but your mother does like to try and make us all feel useful."

Jamie snorted and rose. He pushed his chair back under the kitchen table, as did Vanessa. It was clearly a well-trained reflex. Vanessa reached for Topher's chair.

"I've got it." He gave her hand another squeeze before tucking his own chair under the table. She didn't let go. If anything, her grip tightened. Topher wasn't going to complain. It had been too long since he'd held hands with someone, and the warm contact was comforting.

The downside, if it could be called that, was that it made him all the more aware of Vanessa. The subtle scent of lilac that followed her everywhere. The way her hair wisped around her face. The classy drape of her clothing that made it clear the outfit was expensive, despite the simple lines.

Vanessa's father shot a finger at Topher. "Once we're settled outside, since Martha isn't letting us sneak a slice of whatever you brought yet, I'd love to hear more about your bakery."

Topher nodded. "Sure. It's one of my favorite subjects."

"Dad."

"Oh, Vanessa, lighten up. It's a conversation. I'm not giving him the third degree." The unspoken "yet" hung in the air.

Topher took a deep breath to settle the sudden rampage of mustangs in his stomach. He'd talked about his business to a lot of people. He'd talked to the parents of women he'd dated, too. Why was it that this impending conversation suddenly seemed a lot more important?

And he and Vanessa weren't even dating.

Yet.

11

Vanessa lay in her bed and stared at the ceiling fan as it slowly circled overhead. If she was objective, the previous evening had gone well. She wasn't managing objective.

Every memory caused a tiny cringe.

Her father's not-so-subtle interview, as if Topher was auditioning for a starring role as Vanessa's husband.

Her mother's gleaming looks every time she spied Vanessa's hand in Topher's.

She squeezed her eyes shut.

She'd held his hand. All. Night.

Vanessa rolled over and buried her head under the pillow. She didn't even like him. He was an irritating, obnoxious know-it-all . . . who had come to her rescue like some kind of knight on a unicorn.

Holding his hand had been nice. Comforting.

Natural.

Her phone buzzed on her nightstand.

Vanessa sighed and pushed herself up so she could grab it.

Her mother.

Of course.

"Hi, Mom."

"Are you still asleep? Vanessa, it's after seven."

On a Saturday. After having spent until nine thirty the previous night at their house, followed by a three hour drive home. She only opened the shop for a half-day on Saturdays. At nine. "I was just getting up."

"Hmm. You looked lovely last night."

"Thanks, Mom. So did you. As always." Vanessa rubbed her eyes and threw her legs over the side of the bed. If she was going to have a conversation with her mother, she needed to not be half-asleep. The coffee she'd prepped the night before beckoned with its siren scent from the kitchen. "I thought the dinner party went well. It was lovely to see everyone in a smaller setting."

"You're right, I should have more intimate gatherings. It was much more pleasant. Did your brother tell you he's agreed to step in at your father's company?"

"No. He didn't mention it. I'll call him later to congratulate him." And ask what in the world he was thinking. Although, Jamie's interests and degrees were much more in line with the government consulting Dad's company did. Maybe this was a good move. "Will he live out there? Somewhere closer to DC?"

"That's really between James and your father. I believe the position is mostly remote, so he can do what makes sense as long as he's willing to travel to meet with customers when necessary." Her mother cleared her throat. "Anyway, that's not really why I called."

Vanessa pulled down her largest mug and poured coffee into it. Automatic timers were one of the greatest inventions in history. "Oh? What's up?"

"We enjoyed meeting Topher last night—though I do wish he had a normal name."

"Mom."

"Well, I do. Honestly, people don't need nicknames. You certainly don't *name* someone a nickname. It leaves no room for growth. Anyway, that's not the point. Your father and I are very pleased and hope that the two of you will join us at the Founder's Ball this year."

Vanessa winced. The Founder's Ball was one of the most annoying society events her parents attended. "I don't know, Mom. Where is it being held?"

"That's actually one of the reasons I thought you'd be excited to come. It's at that place you're always raving about—turkey something. Or swan? Some kind of bird."

"Peacock Hill?" Vanessa had mentioned the ball in passing to Claire during one of their conversations. Looked like she'd gone ahead and sent in an application. Good for her.

"It's quite an honor for them to be selected, as I'm sure you know. From what I understand they put together an impressive bid. I'm looking forward to finally having a chance to see the place. I'd like it more if you were there to give me the tour."

She sighed. Her mother tried. This was an olive branch, of sorts. A way for her mom to reach across the chasm that otherwise seemed to grow with every passing year. Vanessa didn't fit into the mold her mom had in mind for her and probably never would. The best thing—maybe even the right one—would be to agree to go. But . . . Topher. "Couldn't you and I go together? You know Dad hates putting on his tux."

Her mother laughed. "Oh, he makes a fuss, but he doesn't actually mind. Besides, how often do you and Topher actually make time for a nice night out?"

"Never." Because they weren't dating. Why couldn't she tack that on and end the charade? "Let me talk to Topher and see what he has to say, okay?"

"Wonderful! We're going to have the best time. I've already sent you an email with all the details. Your father and I are happy to pick up your tickets, so all you have to do is come up with a raffle offering and show up."

"Mom—that's assuming Topher isn't busy." Or somehow saner than she was and would say no. "Don't buy the tickets just yet. Okay?"

"Fine. Let me know soon though, I hate for it to look like we aren't going to attend."

"Why don't you and Dad go ahead and buy yours? I can get ours if Topher can come." They were pricey, but it'd be doable. Maybe she could even write off some of the expense—there was a lot of business networking at events like this.

"I hate to do that to you."

Vanessa smiled. "It's fine. I'll call Topher today and see what I can do. You get your tickets."

"Okay. I do want you to come, Vanessa, you know that, right?"

"I know. I love you, Mom."

"You, too. Let me know soon."

Vanessa pressed end and lowered her head to the kitchen table. Now what? Obviously, she had to call Topher. But then what? Did she ask him to come? Or beg him to give her an excuse? Or . . . she sat up and tapped her fingers on her mug. Call Claire and get the scoop.

Vanessa grabbed her phone and found Claire's number, then waited as it rang.

"Hey, Vanessa. You were on my list to call today—you'll never guess my news!"

"You're hosting the Founder's Ball?"

Silence. Then a laugh. "Yeah. How'd you know that? We were notified on Monday."

Monday? That was late notice if they were already sending out invites. Or was her mother on some kind of early notice list?

Knowing Mom, that was likely. "Still. Congratulations. I didn't even know you'd applied."

"It seemed like a good idea at the time." Claire laughed. "Now everyone here is panicking. We have a solid six weeks—that should be plenty of time, right?"

"I mean, maybe. How much of the event planning are you responsible for? You're just the venue, so what, you clean and let them in to decorate?"

Claire cleared her throat. "It's a little more than that. They gave us guidelines for the decorations, but the implementation is on us. I might have listed you as a potential flower vendor."

Of course she had. And there was no doubt at all in Vanessa's mind that was behind her mother's early morning call. She'd probably find some way to take credit for it—or at least get some recognition out of the fact that her daughter provided the flowers. On the flip side, it was a real coup and if Vanessa pulled it off well. It was an entrée into another aspect of the floral business she'd yet to break into. "Then I guess we need to set up a consult."

"Sure. Why don't I send you everything they sent me about the decorations and you can get back to me about that. At least they're handling the catering. I guess that's a separate bid and highly desired."

Would Topher have sought that out? Maybe he'd legitimately have a conflict. The tightness in her chest loosened with the thought. Even if it wasn't for sure, the prospect of a silver lining was encouraging. "That is good news. Although I imagine you've met enough caterers in the year you've been open you have a pretty good idea who could handle it."

Claire grunted. "I have a list of people I wouldn't approach. Not quite the same thing, but close."

Vanessa laughed. She had a list a lot like that as well. Wedding coordinators she tried to avoid because they let their brides run rampant and make changes at the last minute, then took it out on the contractors. Stopping that madness was the job of the event planner as far as Vanessa was concerned.

"Anyway. If you can do the flowers, I'd love it. I'll tell you up front that we went a little lower on the price than maybe we should have in order to look competitive, but getting weddings or other events for this crowd? Worth it."

"It's great exposure, for sure. Send me the info, and I'll get back to you as quickly as I can. Anything else happening over there?"

"Nah. We have a couple of youth group weekends coming up —fall retreat type stuff—pretty low key on our end. No more weddings booked until next spring. But I've got a line on a small writer's conference and possibly some writing retreats, so that's another possible avenue."

"What's the difference between a writing retreat and a writing conference?"

"No idea. But the ladies I've talked to seem to think they're different. They should be sending me some info next week. Between you and me?"

"Of course." Seriously. Who was she going to tell? Even if she did accidentally blab something about Peacock Hill, it was unlikely to make it to ears that would care.

"I think we're going to be running at capacity by March. Weddings are one-offs. I mean, it's not like people book a wedding every year."

Vanessa laughed. "At least we hope not."

"Right." Claire snickered. "And if they do, I'm not sure they'd keep coming back to the same place that did so poorly for them in the first place. Point being—weddings aren't necessarily reliable annual business. But retreats? The people we had in the spring and summer are already in touch about booking again for this coming year. So there isn't a ton of room when it comes to adding events anyway. This keeps up? I'm not going to have much of a job."

"Oh, now, Claire—I don't think that's true. Even if it's managing recurring bookings, they're always going to need you. Who else would do it?"

"Deidre could. Easy." Claire's gusty sigh crackled in Vanessa's ear. "And since we're basically renovated, it's not like she has all that much else to do. Sure, fix a toilet now and then—stuff like that. But that's not a full time job either."

Vanessa's mind spun. Did Deidre know her sister was talking like this? Thinking like this? She couldn't. Could she? "Have you talked to your sister?"

"No. And you aren't going to, either. Promise me."

She winced. "Okay. But I think you should. With the baby coming, she's for sure not going to want you leaving."

"The baby isn't due until the end of January. Or early February. There's time. So I guess we'll see." Vanessa could picture Claire's one-shouldered shrug. Claire cleared her throat. "So. The Founder's Ball?"

"Get me the info. I'll get back to you fast."

"Thanks, Vanessa."

"Sure. Bye." Vanessa ended the call and frowned at her phone. Putting off calling Topher wasn't cowardice. She had to wait and see if she was doing the flowers. It wasn't like she could attend and . . . yeah okay, she couldn't even con herself with that one. She'd done flowers for events she'd attended plenty of times. All her work was beforehand.

She gulped down the rest of her coffee and rose to fill her mug again.

She'd get ready and go down to open the shop. If she had some extra time, she'd call Topher.

It wasn't procrastinating.

It was being practical.

12

"Why don't you just go in to work?" Brian muted the TV and frowned across the room.

Topher jangled the change in his pocket. "They don't need me. Closing soon anyway."

"Go for a run then. Or, I don't know, fishing."

Topher snorted. "Fishing?"

Brian tossed his hands in the air. "I don't know what you do for fun, man. All I ever see you do is go to work, or events, and then crash on the couch either with a book or the TV."

And that, right there, was an entirely too accurate picture of his life. Accurate and depressing. "You're what, the cruise director now? What have you done other than go to the office and mope lately?"

"So . . . you want to fight?" Brian sighed and clicked the TV off. "Okay. What about?"

"I don't *know*."

"My choice then. Hmm."

Topher fought a grin and lost. "Jerk."

"Yeah, okay. Name calling usually works. Moron."

Topher laughed and sank into a chair. He scrubbed his hands over his face.

"Call her."

"And say what?"

"Ask her out. On a real date, not some dinner at her parents' house. Take her to dinner. Tonight, even."

There was nothing Topher would like better than that. It was unlikely she'd go. "She held my hand. All night."

"I repeat: call her and ask her out."

"I just don't think—"

"Stop thinking. Start dialing. Seriously, man, if you're going to obsess all afternoon, you might as well find out if you're wasting your time. What's the worst thing that could happen?"

She could say no. Tell him she had less than zero interest in him. Explain that she still hated his guts and found him insufferable. Variations on that theme. And? So what? It wasn't as if he hadn't experienced rejection before. No man who'd tried to date in his lifetime escaped unscathed.

"You'll never know if you don't ask." Brain turned the TV back on. "By the way, I should be out of your hair at the end of the month. I found a basement apartment."

Topher blinked. He'd gotten used to having Brian around. It wasn't as if he didn't have the space for a roommate. "You didn't have to do that."

Brian shrugged. "I think we'd all be better off if I got back to my life. You're not the only one with a stalled-out love life."

Ah. He'd hoped Brian was thinking about some of the conversations they'd had about his lifestyle. About Jesus. Maybe he was. "I'll miss having you around."

Brian chuckled. "I'll still be around. I miss the rest of my crowd though, they're my people. I know you get that at some level. But even though we run in completely different circles, you've never made me feel other. I appreciate it."

"You're my friend, Bri."

He held up a hand. "Before you get all weepy, go call this woman. If I can see you settled in a relationship before I go, it'll give me hope."

"No pressure, though, right?"

"Please. There's pressure. A lot of it." Brian winked. "Don't let me down."

Topher's stomach gave a greasy twist. He took a long breath in through his nose and let it out. "Thanks. Helpful."

He strode upstairs before Brian could respond. The last thing Topher needed was more of his friend's "encouragement."

Should he call Vanessa? He'd basically promised Brian he would. Which meant . . . Topher slipped his phone out of his pocket and stared at it.

"Here we go." He blew out a breath and tapped Vanessa's contact before he could talk himself out of it.

"This is Vanessa."

Topher's eyebrows lifted. What did it mean that she didn't recognize his number? Or have it saved? Did it mean anything, or was he over thinking? Again. He cleared his throat. "Hi, Vanessa. It's Topher."

"Oh. Topher. Hi."

Not the most encouraging greeting, as such things went. A ball of hot lead lodged in his chest. This was a bad idea. Could he come up with an easy excuse for calling and hang up? His mind blanked. "Um. I just wanted to say thanks for letting me join you for dinner last night."

She laughed. "I'm not sure 'let you' is the right phrase. My mom really didn't leave you a choice. I appreciate you being flexible enough to come along. It was over and above."

"I had fun. I like your family." Topher closed his eyes. Why did he say that? It was true, sure, but Vanessa's relationship with them was clearly strained. Would he ever learn to keep his mouth shut?

"You really mean that?"

"Actually, yeah. I do."

"Hmm. Have you ever heard of the Founder's Ball?"

"I don't think so. I don't usually try for big society events though—weddings, church stuff, maybe a one-day conference—those are more my speed. I had a friend try to convince me to apply for some of the Gold Cup shindigs. I took one look at the application and spent a week laughing."

Vanessa snorted. "My mother loves the Gold Cup."

Of course she did. Foot, meet mouth. Again. "Sorry."

"Oh, no. I happen to agree with you completely. I mean, the horses are beautiful, and there's not much better than being out in the rolling Virginia hills on a nice, spring day. But the rest of it? No, thank you. Still, the Founder's Ball isn't quite that bad."

"Who's the founder and what did he found? Find? Found. He would have founded something, right?"

Her laughter soothed the nerves that were starting to crawl along the inside of his skin. Where had her annoying giggle gone? Had she changed, or had he? "Huh. I'm not actually sure. My parents have been going for years, and I have no idea."

"Well, is there an auction or something? Usually these things have some big fundraiser attached, right?"

"A raffle, yeah."

"Where do the proceeds go?" Surely that would explain who the Founder was. Or at least what had been founded.

"It varies. Last year was the children's hospital in Charlottesville. The year before was some wildlife rescue. They take applications and choose something each year."

"Interesting. So much for that idea. It doesn't matter, I guess. I was just curious. So, why'd you ask?"

"Why'd I ask what?"

"If I'd heard of it."

"Oh. Right. My parents go every year. I think I said that. Anyway, Mom was hoping we'd go with them this year. You and me."

His heart lifted. She was asking him out? Even better. "To the ball."

"Yeah. Look, I know it's an imposition. You can say no. At least then I can tell my mother I tried and you were busy. They were really excited that they thought I had a boyfriend, and I know that's absolutely not your problem. I should've set Mom straight before you had to deal with dinner last night, but I couldn't figure out how. I'm sorry."

"When is it?" Topher put the call on speaker and flipped to his calendar app. Better not to try and process that whole explosion of information. She wasn't interested in him. Her mother was. Wasn't that dandy? He was the idea of a relationship rather than actual relationship material.

"November second. It's a Saturday. But really, Topher, I only told my mom I'd ask. You can say no."

"Do you want me to say no?" He bit his lip.

"It'd be easier if you didn't. But—"

"I don't have anything scheduled on the second. I can go. Who knows, it could be fun. Where is it?"

"Peacock Hill. You sound—I don't know, annoyed."

"Why would I be annoyed?"

"I don't know. I'm asking. I . . . this is dumb. I'll just tell my mother you're busy."

"But I'm not busy."

Vanessa let out a short scream.

"Email me the info."

She sighed. "Are you sure?"

He was the exact opposite of sure. In fact, he was reasonably convinced this was one of his stupidest decisions. "Of course. You said your mom thinks we're dating?"

There was a long pause before Vanessa's voice whispered across the line. "Yeah."

"Then we should probably go out some between now and then as well. Make it convincing."

"No. Topher—she knows I'm busy. My shop, your shop. They're good excuses."

"Not really. Not if we're a couple. It might fly for a while, but long term? It'll cause more problems than it solves. Lunch tomorrow after church?" Why was he pushing this? Probably because he needed his head examined.

"I—we—it's—yeah, all right. Maybe Sean and Larissa could join us?"

"Let's see what happens. You're hitting the ten thirty service again?"

"That's the plan, yeah."

"Okay. I'll meet you in the foyer. See you tomorrow." Toper ended the call and tossed his phone on his bed. What was wrong with him?

Vanessa clearly had no interest in him. So now, not only had he horned in on a dinner at her parents' house, but he'd forced her into some sort of made-up relationship, culminating in a black tie event at the start of the holiday season.

And for what, exactly?

TOPHER SCANNED the crowd in the church foyer. Vanessa should be here by now. He'd seen Sean and Larissa already—they'd gone in to grab seats. Was she coming? Maybe she'd come to her senses and—he stopped that train of thought. She could have said no. The Founder's Ball, for that matter, had been her idea.

All he'd done was buy himself a little bit of time to convince her that he was someone worth getting to know. Given how badly they usually got along at events, this was his chance.

So he wasn't going to blow it.

There she was.

Topher lifted his hand and smiled when her gaze met his. Pink tinged her cheeks as she wove through the thinning clumps of people.

"Hi. Sorry." She clutched her Bible to her chest, a little out of breath. "Are you ready to go in?"

"Yeah. Sean and Larissa were going to try and save us seats."

"Oh." Vanessa paused. "Okay."

What did that mean? Hadn't hanging out with them been her idea? "We don't have to sit with them. They'll understand."

"No. No, it's fine." She blew out a breath and stopped, turning to face him. "You were trying to ask me out. On a date. Right?"

Topher nodded.

"But just to make the thing at the ball convincing."

He lifted a shoulder. At some point, self-preservation had to kick in, didn't it? Laying it all on the line was one thing. Doing it more than once? That was for suckers.

"What does that mean? It's a yes or no question, Topher."

The praise band kicked off the first song and he reached for the sanctuary door. "Come on, we don't want to be late."

"But—"

"We can talk about it later."

Vanessa scowled at him, but she snapped her mouth shut and started down the aisle.

Topher scanned for Sean and Larissa. Maybe having them as a buffer wasn't a bad idea. Especially if Vanessa was going back to being touchy and hard to understand.

What was it with her?

At her parents' house, and during the long drive there and back, she'd been this woman who Topher couldn't wait to get to know better. He'd already seen glimpses of that—it was why he'd been at her shop in the first place when her mother mistook him for more than he was.

My Topher.

It might have been a slip—it obviously had been a slip—but Vanessa's words stuck with him. He wanted them to be true.

That probably made him a fool. But he still couldn't help wanting more.

13

V anessa stood as the band filed back on stage. Hardly any of the pastor's words had made it through the buzzing in her head. Drat Topher.

She glanced at Topher and frowned. His eyes were closed as he sang. Why did he have to be handsome? And have a passable singing voice? Couldn't he have warts or croak like a toad— something that would make it easier to shrug off his attention and come clean to her mother about their relationship status? Or serious lack thereof.

Her stomach was in knots as she dragged her attention back to the words projected on the two screens up front.

He wanted them to eat lunch together. Was it a date? Fake date? Or were they going out to make things look convincing? That had to be it.

She'd run through the conversation with him so many times since they'd ended their phone call the night before and still didn't have an answer. His weird little half-shrug before the service hadn't made it any clearer.

How much did it matter?

Her parents expected them to be at the Founder's Ball

together. Topher had agreed to go. Why couldn't that be enough?

Sure, maybe it made sense to spend a little more time together between now and then—but it was six weeks away. There had to be at least three events during that time. Wouldn't that count?

Topher's hand was warm on her elbow. "You okay?"

"Yeah. Of course." She forced her lips to curve. Had she heard any of the service? Apparently not. She leaned around him to wave at Larissa and Sean. "Hi, guys."

Larissa's eyes danced with laughter. "Hi. It's good to see you."

"Would you like to join us for lunch?" Better to ask before they had a chance to escape. Or Topher said something that would get them to decline. She and Topher weren't dating. Not for real. If he wasn't going to explain what he thought about it, it was better to make her expectations clear.

"Oh, sorry." Larissa frowned and turned to glance at Sean a moment before turning back to Vanessa. "We're meeting Sean's parents at their country club."

Sean faked a snore. "Believe me, if we'd known there was another option, we would have bailed."

Topher chuckled. "Another time, then. It's good to spend time with your parents, though. We had dinner with Vanessa's folks on Friday—it was fun."

Vanessa cleared her throat and ignored Larissa's raised eyebrows.

Sean pointed at Topher. "Text me later, and let me know when we can get together for coffee. There are some—you know what? Just text me."

"Sure. Okay. Or you can swing by the shop. We serve coffee. And amazing pastries." Topher slid his hand around to rest lightly on Vanessa's lower back. He glanced down at her. "You're still okay for lunch?"

She could make something up. An appointment. Phone call. Something. Except it would be a lie. As little as she wanted to date Topher, she didn't want to lie. "Yeah."

Topher grinned. "Great. How do you feel about tapas?"

Vanessa blinked. Tapas. Little plates designed for sharing. "I . . . I've never really thought about it."

"It's a lot of fun. And delicious. Plus you get to try all kinds of different things, so it's more fun than a big plate of the same old. Game?"

She met his challenging stare and swallowed. Was he daring her? Were they ten? She didn't need to give in to that kind of ridiculous behavior. Vanessa opened her mouth to suggest a more traditional, normal chain restaurant. "Bring it."

Wait. What? No.

"Excellent. We could leave your car here, and I'll bring you back?"

She shook her head. "I'll meet you there."

Temporary insanity might have made her lose the restaurant battle, but that didn't mean she was going to lose the war.

"Okay. I'll text you the address so you don't get lost."

Get lost? She'd lived in Richmond for the bulk of her adult life. Not that she knew where to find a tapas restaurant, but she could Google with the best of them. "Sure. Whatever."

Topher shot her a confused look before tapping at his phone. After a moment, her phone chimed. "It's about twenty minutes from here, depending on the lights."

"Okay. I'm sure I'll find it." Vanessa fought the urge to roll her eyes. She was a grown woman who navigated the roads every day without a problem. Why was he making this weird?

"Right." Topher tucked his hands in his pockets. "So, I'll see you there?"

Something in his tone made her glance up. A hint of vulnerability flitted at the edges of his expression. Oh. The tightness in her chest loosened and she stepped closer, holding his gaze. "I'll be right behind you the whole way."

His eyes searched her face before he nodded. "'K. Where'd you park?"

Vanessa pointed vaguely toward the front lot.

"I'll drive around and meet you at your spot? Then we can go from there."

She nodded and started toward the door. It was a bit of overkill—he'd texted her the address—but if he was that worried about her not showing, she didn't mind following him to ease his mind.

Before long, they were winding their way through the streets of Richmond. This wasn't an area she frequented. Vanessa would have been relying heavily on the GPS if she'd been on her own. One thing she could say though, Topher was good at leading. He didn't careen through yellow lights. He remembered to use his turn signal and changed lanes when there was enough space for them both to get over. She hadn't paid much attention to his driving when they went to her parents' house—but maybe the fact that it didn't stand out meant he'd been just as conscientious then as he was now.

Had she found the only good driver in Virginia?

She chuckled to herself and signaled before sliding behind Topher at the curb in front of what looked like a row of town homes. Was something wrong?

Topher tapped on her window.

Vanessa pressed the button to lower it. "Are we lost after all?"

"No." He grinned and pointed to a path, edged on both sides with chain link fencing, that led behind the town homes. "It's just through there. There's never enough parking. Especially not on a Sunday. The residents here don't mind."

"You're sure?" Street parking in neighborhoods in the city could be tricky. "No permit required?"

He shook his head.

All right. With a mental shrug, Vanessa rolled up her window, shut off the engine, and grabbed her purse. She pushed open the car door and stood. "Lead the way."

THE TINY TABLE near the kitchen where they'd been seated by the elated owner of the hole-in-the-wall restaurant was stacked with empty plates. Vanessa leaned back, her stomach pleasantly full, and smiled.

"You have room for dessert?"

"Oh. I don't think so." She resisted the urge to pat her belly. "What were you going to recommend?"

Topher laughed—a sound she was not only getting used to hearing, but one she looked forward to. "I don't know. I figured Sophia would have a recommendation."

Sophia was the owner. Vanessa had pieced that much together. She adored Topher. That was also clear. "How do you know the family again?"

"I've helped with several events for them. Mostly they do their own catering—you can see why—but sometimes someone wants desserts that are more formal or French-inspired than what the d'Avilas generally make. Then they call me." He shrugged. "We've gotten to be friends. I think Sophia has nine children? They're all busy with families of their own. So there are lots of parties—weddings, sure, but birthdays, anniversaries, what have you. They make a party out of them all. I'm not sure if that's because they're from Spain, or they just love parties."

Looking around, Vanessa suspected it was the latter. The little restaurant was full and every table seemed to be a miniature party in its own right. How much of that was the influence of the owners? "Sounds like a fun job."

"Always. What about you? Have a favorite client who keeps coming back?"

Did she? There were regulars, sure. Did she look forward to seeing any of them? Would she seek out their business to return the favor? "Oh! I know. Mr. Singleton. He comes in every other Wednesday to get flowers for his wife. They've been married going on sixty years now."

"I like that. What would it be for you?"

Vanessa frowned. "What do you mean?"

"Well, flowers would be ridiculous. And you don't care for sweets. So what would your husband bring you routinely to let you know how much he still loved you?"

Vanessa reached for her glass and took a gulp of the icy water. "I like flowers. Just because I work with them doesn't mean I don't appreciate them."

"Uh-huh. But they're not special."

"They can be." What did he want from her? She sighed. "Chocolate covered almonds. Dark chocolate."

"Seriously?" He grinned. "Like almond bark?"

"Sure. That's good too. But the individual ones where the chocolate is all glossy? Those are my favorite."

"But you don't eat sweets."

"Well—that's different. Sort of. It's not cake or anything."

"Relax. I'm giving you a hard time."

"I did appreciate the cupcakes. And the fruit tart. You have a real gift with pastry. I guess I didn't figure you needed me to tell you that."

He offered a tiny smile. "Apparently I did. Thanks."

"This was fun."

"You sound surprised."

"I am. A little." Vanessa shrugged. "Sorry."

"Don't be. We had a rocky start."

She snorted. "That's an understatement."

"Maybe a tiny one. Oh, hey, I looked up the Founder's Ball—swanky. How'd the Peacock Hill gang grab it?"

"I mentioned it as something to apply for, but beyond that? It was all Claire. She's a whiz with stuff like that." Should she mention that Claire sounded unhappy—restless? No. Not her place. And what would Topher be able to do about it anyway? If he was friends with anyone out there, it'd be the guys. "I may end up doing the flowers. Claire asked me for a proposal."

"Yeah?" A grin split his face. "That's amazing. Congrats."

"It's not a done deal yet." Her face heated. "I'll do it for them, but honestly? Networking with that kind of crowd isn't really my scene."

"Too close to home?"

Why did he understand it so well? No one else did. "Yeah."

"I still think it'd be great for you. You'd still be able to attend?"

Vanessa nodded. And maybe, with Topher along, she'd manage to enjoy it.

"Did you get your tickets?"

Vanessa didn't bother to sigh. "Not yet. I'll do it today, Mom."

"What's the holdup? Can't Topher come? Are you sure I can't get them for you?"

"He can. He is. We are. I just got home from church. I really don't mind buying them."

"It's nearly four o'clock. What church are you going to?"

"Topher and I went to lunch after the service."

"Ah. I'm glad to hear that. You get so busy with your business, I'm sure it impacts your ability to sustain a relationship. That's always been the excuse you've given, at least."

Vanessa closed her eyes and sank back into her couch. Was

there any point in counting? Ten wasn't going to be high enough. Neither would a hundred. At some point she'd have to speak again and then her mother would respond and she'd be back to counting from one again. "Did you just call to ask about the tickets?"

"I didn't want you to forget. You know you do that."

Only to get out of things that held no interest. Vanessa wrinkled her nose. She'd thought she was getting away with that. Apparently not so much. "Sorry. I'll take care of the tickets as soon as we're off the phone."

"And then text me."

"And then I'll text you."

"When will you know if you've been selected as the floral vendor for the ball?"

She shook her head. Did her mother know everything? "How'd you find out about that?"

"I may not sit on the committee, but I have friends who do. They mentioned you were part of the Peacock Hill application. It worked in their favor somewhat."

Somewhat. That was a loaded term. One she had no intention of exploring. "I sent Claire details last night. If it's within her price—or if I can make it work—we'll go from there."

"That sounds less certain than I expected. You don't think you'll be doing the flowers?"

"No, I do. I want to, at least, and made it clear that I'll wiggle as much as I can. It's a matter of making sure Claire and I have the same vision."

Her mother sniffed. "I'd think you would have a better picture of what that should be. You've been attending this ball since you were eighteen."

When she'd agreed to go only to get her mother to stop pressuring her to attend the Debutante's Ball in New York City. Their family wasn't old money—no matter how much Mom liked to pretend they were. Vanessa had no interest in feeding that fantasy. "Which is why I suspect Claire will be on board with my proposal, but we'll have to wait and see. I imagine she'll get back with me tomorrow."

"How hard is it? You should follow up today."

"They don't work on Sunday. I'm trying not to. And if it was any other potential client, you'd be supportive of that."

"You're right. I'm sorry. I'm excited. This is a real feather in your cap, Vanessa. Think of the families who will be there and the connections you might make."

The same families she'd been rubbing elbows with every year. "Everyone already knows I'm a florist, Mom."

"Yes, but now they'll get to see your work in person. That's so much nicer than looking online or visiting your little shop."

"I'm not sure what I'd do with more square footage. I've got a good-sized work area in the back and ample room in front for client pickup or walk-ins. What do you feel like I'm missing?"

"I'm sure I don't know. Why would you even ask?"

"You're always commenting on the size—calling it my little shop. I assumed that meant you felt I needed something larger, but I honestly can't see what I'd do with more space." Vanessa pressed her lips together. She should've stopped the words before they came out. There was no point regretting them now. Honestly though, did her mother not understand how condescending she was?

Her mother's voice was stiff. "I apologize. I didn't mean to imply your space was inadequate."

Not the space, no, just the rest of the venture. And possibly Vanessa as well. "Thank you. I'm sure if you do have concerns you could talk to Dad. He was quite pleased with the building when I first looked, before I bought it. And the bonus of being able to live above the shop and owning both parts can't be overstated."

"Yes, I'm sure. But what about when you marry? Where will you live then? Surely you don't mean to try and raise a family above your flower shop?"

"That's a long way off and not something I'm worrying about right now." Topher had a townhouse, didn't he? They could live there and . . . what was she thinking? She wasn't even in a relationship with Topher. Why would he be the person who came to mind?

"You and Topher haven't talked about it? Aren't you serious about him? These are conversations you need to have before you're engaged. You know this. Does he want children? Will he support you closing the flower shop to raise those children?"

"Whoa. Who said anything about closing my shop? There are plenty of women who run a business and are still involved mothers. Besides, Topher and I aren't anywhere near the 'what happens after we marry' conversation. We're not even really—"

"Oh, honey, you need to have these conversations early and often. Your father and I probably didn't talk about the what-ifs quite as much as we should have. There were some rocky days the first several years that we probably could have avoided if we'd spent more time before we were married thinking things through."

Vanessa frowned and adjusted the phone. She'd never noticed her parents having trouble. If anything, they seemed to her to have two separate lives that happened to be going on under the same roof. They were too disinterested in one another to have bumpy spots. Weren't they? "I'll keep that in mind."

"Do that. It's okay for you to bring up, you know. You don't have to wait for Topher to decide to mention it." Her mother sighed. "I do wish he had a real name."

She smothered her chuckle. "He does, Mom. It's Topher."

"Yes, and that's a lovely nickname. If you're the sort of person who needs or wants one of those. Do you think he'd mind terribly if I called him Christopher?"

"Given that it's not his name, I imagine it might be a tad off-putting, yes. Besides, I don't know that you're going to have all that much time to call him anything. We aren't really in a relationship."

"Oh, please. I realize your generation isn't into defining things like mine was—that's not new. My mother was constantly asking who I was going steady with in high school and that simply wasn't a term we used. We went out or were boyfriend and girlfriend. Going steady seemed so antiquated. But he took you to lunch. He came to the house. He's escorting you to the ball. You're dating. It's a good step toward meeting the new terms of your trust. Although, between you and me, your father is considering letting that go now that he's met Topher."

"Even if it doesn't work out?" Because after the Founder's Ball, she and Topher would have no more reason to pretend to have a relationship. She wasn't using him to get to the money—a year ago, she might have considered it. Not anymore. So now what? Did she have to convince him to stage a break up to get her mother to believe they were through? She'd finally managed to say the words and Mom, in her typical fashion, had rolled right over her. Was she supposed to push harder?

"Tsk. So negative. He's clearly smitten with you. I don't understand why you have to fly to worst case extremes. Your birthday isn't that far off, you know, and I suspect as long as you're in a relationship with Topher at the time your father will take that as an intention to marry."

Vanessa pressed her fingers against her eyelids. "It's okay if he doesn't. I've gotten used to the idea that I won't be getting any more money. My business meets my needs."

"I wonder if Topher would be so quick to toss it away."

"He doesn't know about the trust."

"Vanessa! Do the two of you have any conversations that matter?"

Before this afternoon? No. No, they had not. And even today hadn't been full of deep revelation, for all she had a better handle on who Topher was as a man. He was a good one. A godly one. The kind of man she'd never be able to deserve.

Her mom started in before she could respond. "You need to do better. It isn't as if you've never had a solid relationship. That boy in college—you were with him for what, three years? Surely the two of you had conversations about your future and prospects."

"Ricky." Vanessa swallowed the lump in her throat. She and Ricky had indeed had those talks. Then when he'd discovered she didn't get to keep the first round of her trust money—that she intended to follow tradition and set up a foundation—he'd started looking around for someone new. She'd known it. Seen it. But she hadn't been willing to let go. So he'd made it impossible for her to do otherwise by getting caught making out with her roommate. Because why not ruin two relationships in one shot and really make the point? "We did. And you see how well that worked out."

"Richard. Right. Your father never did like him."

That was news. "He never said."

"You seemed committed, so he tried. Anyway, it doesn't matter. He does like Topher—as do I—so make sure you do what you can to hold on to him. I have to run. I'd like to take you shopping for a dress for the ball. If you're willing. It would be fun."

That would be an all-day affair that probably involved a drive into DC or at least Alexandria, because her mother didn't seem to think Richmond had clothing stores. "I planned to look locally, but I appreciate the thought."

"I can come to you. Let me know if you decide you'd like that." There was an undercurrent of hurt in her mother's voice.

Vanessa bit her lip. "Let me look at my schedule and see if I can take a day off."

"Okay. Thank you. I love you, Vanessa."

"Love you too, Mom." She tapped end and dropped her phone on the couch. She'd forgotten all about the dress-shoes-bag aspect of the ball. Just another layer of the event that held no interest. But, if she was going to do the flowers, attending and having the chance to talk to people in person would be worth it. It had to be. Because otherwise the costs for this fiasco in the making were starting to add up: new fancy dress, accompanying fancy shoes and purse, the tickets themselves.

And, oh yes, best of all, a fake relationship with Topher.

14

Topher scrubbed down the final countertop in the kitchen of his bakery and wrung out the sponge. Everyone else had left while he finished up. They'd offered to stay as they always did, but the quiet was nice. He checked the back door locks before moving up front to ensure they'd cleaned and straightened everything so it was ready for the next day.

Friday mornings were always a rush. Anything he could do Thursday evening was a bonus. The three tables he had shoe-horned against the front window sparkled in the sinking sunlight. Chairs were wiped and tucked away. Even the display case gleamed.

They barely needed him anymore.

He sighed and tucked his hands in his pockets. That was why he'd expanded into wedding cakes. The bakery itself was a fairly well-oiled machine. His kitchen staff could handle all the recipes—had even improved on several of them. The counter staff was courteous and knew the regulars by name. Something he'd once been able to do but now? Only the folks who'd been coming since the beginning were even familiar.

Should he step back more completely?

He could take on more weddings if he did that. Not that he was turning anyone away right now. The fall was always slower on the wedding front. There were still events—anniversaries, birthdays, that sort of thing. Plus, Thanksgiving would be here before long and then Christmas. The shop's pies always sold out over the holidays.

Topher made a mental note to update the website with seasonal order information. It wasn't too early for some party planners, and people today seemed to appreciate not having to pick up the phone and talk to a live human being.

Whereas he enjoyed that. Looked forward to it.

Was anxious to call one of them in particular.

Vanessa.

Shaking his head, he unlocked the front door and pushed through it, hitting the lights as he stepped out. He relocked the shop and gave the door a jiggle to ensure the locks had caught. Her shop wasn't closed for the day yet.

Muttering to himself, he got in his car and pulled out into traffic. It was stupid to drop by. He should just call.

And say what?

She was unlikely to care that he'd been thinking about her occasionally. Off and on.

Constantly.

Since Sunday.

Four days without calling or swinging by. That had to count for something, didn't it? It wasn't as if she couldn't have reached out to him if she'd wanted to.

Did that mean she didn't want to?

Their shops weren't so far apart that it took long to arrive. He was parking before he'd mentally prepared. What would he say when she asked why he was there? Because she was going to ask. Topher sighed. He'd wing it.

What could go wrong?

Topher lowered his head to the steering wheel. Was he doing the right thing here? He'd been praying about it. A lot. And he didn't have a solid answer one way or the other. No lightning bolts or angels holding signs telling him, yes, Vanessa was the woman God had for him. On the flip side, there were no tugs in his heart saying he should run in the other direction. He'd felt those before.

So. He'd press on and trust God to either make something solid and real out of this relationship or make it clear this wasn't the right direction.

There were two men and a woman with a stroller in the sales area of Vanessa's shop. That was the busiest Topher had ever seen it. He lifted a hand when the door chimed, and her frantic gaze landed on him.

"Hi, I'll be right—oh, Topher. Hi." Confusion flitted across her face. "Did you need something?"

He shook his head and slid up to the counter. "I just dropped by. Thought you might like dinner."

"I've got another hour and a half here." She blew the wisps of hair that had fallen over her eyes out of the way.

"I can wait." The words slipped out. They weren't wrong—he had nothing else planned tonight—but they sounded a little more pathetic than he'd expected. "Can I help?"

She studied him for several heartbeats before nodding. "Actually, yeah. Both of the gentlemen are looking for something for their wives, but that's about as specific as I've been able to gather. Maybe you can give them a nudge and figure out if it's an occasion or an apology or just because? Then I can dash in the back and finish the table arrangement for the woman whose baby is liable to start screaming any minute. Every time I go in the back, the door chimes."

He grinned. "Got it. Go finish her flowers. I'll hold down the front."

"You're sure?"

"Positive."

Vanessa squeezed his hand. "Thank you."

The warmth from her touch—and her words—spread through him. He winked and crossed to where the two men stood eyeing the pre-made arrangements in the cooler. "Gentlemen. How can I help?"

"YOU DIDN'T HAVE to cook. I was thinking we'd go out." Topher shifted in his seat at Vanessa's kitchen table and glanced around. Her apartment was tidy. And sparsely decorated. What did it say about her that she had only one photo hanging on her wall? It was her brother—though it had to have been several years prior. The rest of the wall hangings were art prints and post cards, all framed.

"It's relaxing. And after the crazy end of the day downstairs, dealing with the crowd at a restaurant didn't appeal. You're sure it's okay?" She shook the pan on the stove before splashing in some soy sauce. "Stir-fry's simple, but I like it."

"Who doesn't?"

Vanessa chuckled. "I could make you a list."

"Takes all kinds, I guess. For me? It's a weekday staple. Long day in the kitchen, there's nothing I want more than a quick, filling meal. Vegetables are a bonus."

She grinned and turned off the stove. In short order, she'd taken down two plates from one of the cabinets and dished up generous portions.

Topher waited while she filled two glasses with water and,

finally, settled in the seat to his left. He offered her his hand. "Can I say grace?"

Vanessa eyed his hand like it might be carrying the plague but finally rested her fingers in his. "Thanks."

He kept the prayer short and to the point, regardless of his desire to hold her hand longer. She was clearly uncomfortable. Topher gave her fingers a quick squeeze as he said, "Amen."

"So." Vanessa stabbed several snow peas and a thin strip of chicken.

Topher waited but she didn't go on. "So, what?"

She laughed. "My brother used to do that."

Topher speared a bite and watched her eat. "How's he doing?"

"I wish I knew. Mom says he took a job with Dad's company."

"Is that a bad thing?"

"No. No, it's probably a good one. His skills and interests mesh well enough with the contracts they've always sought. But he hasn't been in touch, and that worries me. Last time he did that, he disappeared completely for years. I guess I was hoping that since I was his first stop we might be able to reclaim some of the friendship we had when we were younger." Vanessa shrugged, but Topher caught a glimpse of hurt in her eyes before she looked away. "I'm sure he's just busy."

He reached out and covered her hand. When she didn't immediately pull away, he curled his fingers around hers more tightly. "Have you called him? Texted? Emailed?"

"I don't want to be a nag."

Topher swallowed a chuckle. "Since your brother seems like a pretty typical guy, I'm going to let you in on a secret. He'd probably love it if you got in touch with him first."

"I don't know." She tugged her hand away and reached for her water. "Why?"

"You said he disappeared? No contact, right? And he knows you were hurt and worried by that?"

She nodded.

"He's probably embarrassed. And not quite sure how to fix things—or even if you really want things to be fixed."

"I don't see how that could be. I practically told him all of that when he came home. He knows I love him and missed him and am glad he's back."

"Sure. He probably does. But he also probably needs reassurance that you weren't just saying that."

"Men are weird."

Topher laughed. "As compared to women who are so even-keeled and easy to understand."

Vanessa snickered.

He pointed a finger at her. "I heard that."

"While you're being regaled with my family drama, you should know my mother wants to go dress shopping with me. For the ball."

Why was he supposed to care about that? It was obvious Vanessa and her mom had a challenging relationship—from everything he'd observed, most grown women did—but the underpinnings were love. Maybe her mom struggled to see her daughter as a capable adult, and didn't love the choices Vanessa made all the time, but she clearly loved Vanessa. "Okay?"

"It just means I'm liable to end up with something more formal than I'd planned on, which, in turn, means you're stuck with a tuxedo. I'd hoped you'd be able to get by with a nice suit."

"I look good in a tux."

Vanessa raised her eyebrows. "You're not going to complain about a penguin suit?"

"Nah. I don't get a chance to wear mine often enough. It's not like you can just decide to throw that on and go get a burger."

"You own a tuxedo?" She set her fork down with a clink.

"Sure. A lot of guys do. When you're in a ton of weddings, it's easier to have your own than to deal with going to this that or the other rental place where they inevitably measure something wrong and you end up miserable for an evening. So, since generally all that changes is the vest or cummerbund and tie, this was easier. And more cost effective. No tails though. I've never needed tails."

Vanessa looked away.

"Do I need to apologize? I can grump around and rent something if that'll make the experience more realistic for you."

She let out a short laugh. "No. That's okay. I just keep waiting . . . you know what? Never mind. Did I tell you I'm doing the flowers for the ball, too?"

"No, you didn't. That's great! I wasn't actually worried that Claire would choose someone else. Were you?"

Vanessa lifted a shoulder. "Kinda. I mean it's a big deal. I'm sure they gave her a list of vendors who've done it before. This is such a great win for them. I don't want to let them down."

"You won't." His mind circled back to her comment about waiting. What was she waiting for? He obviously couldn't pursue it. Not right now, at least. But there had to be some way to get her to finish the sentence.

"Just like that?"

"Just like that. I've watched you handle flowers for quite a few temperamental brides. Brides whose weddings were over the top elaborate. I don't imagine Claire is going that direction. So you'll do a great job, and it'll be a big bonus for both of you business-wise."

"Are you always this optimistic?"

Topher shook his head.

"All right. Then thanks. You're right about Claire's ideas. They're playing up the peacock theme—makes sense given the carvings and stained glass and, well, peacocks everywhere. I'm kind of looking forward to designing some big standing arrangements that look like peacock tails."

Topher chuckled. That could either be amazing or ridiculous. His money was on amazing. "Can't wait to see them. What time will you need to be down there to setup?"

"I planned to go down early so I had most of the day. I can probably put everything together here, but it might be easier to transport some of the larger arrangements in pieces and assemble them onsite. I won't know until I've firmed up exactly what I'm doing. The ball doesn't start until seven—I can meet you."

"Do you need a hand with the flowers?"

"Maybe. Claire thinks Duncan and Anna will be around. She's going to check. Landscape design isn't completely the same, but they probably still have an eye."

"Let me help."

"I don't want to take you away from your shop."

"They hardly need me. Let me help you." He met and held her gaze. All of the jittery edges inside of him smoothed. "Please?"

"You're sure?"

He nodded.

"Okay." Vanessa looked away.

Topher turned his attention back to the half-finished plate of stir-fry. Emotions swirled around inside him, clogging up somewhere just above his heart. Did she feel anything for him or was he a means to an end?

15

Vanessa pushed the food around on her plate. Her stomach was too tight to eat any more. Why would looking into Topher's eyes have any effect on her? He was obnoxious and overbearing . . . except he wasn't.

Drat the man.

She looked around her apartment. What did he think? She rarely had anyone over. It was her retreat.

"This was delicious. Thank you." Topher set his fork on his plate and pushed away from the table. "Are you finished?"

"Yeah."

He reached for her plate as he stood, then carried them the short distance to the sink. "Where do you keep your containers for leftovers?"

"I'll get it." She stood hastily, her chair tipping back.

Topher opened and shut cabinets. "I like to help. Aha."

Vanessa fought mortification as the recycled containers from deli chicken tumbled out of the cabinet onto the counter.

"Mine always do that, too. It doesn't make sense. They stack inside one another, so you'd think you could do that and they'd stay, but it's like they have a party when the cabinet door shuts or something." Topher grinned and set one container and a lid aside before scooping up the others and shoving them back onto the shelf and closing the door.

"Let me." Vanessa reached for her plate and the container, her fingers brushing over his. His hands were always warm. And softer than they should be. Didn't a baker wash his hands all the time? His skin should be dry and rough.

Topher's smile was easy as he rinsed his plate at the sink and waited, hand outstretched for hers. "Is the dishwasher okay to use?"

"I guess, although I never do. It's just me, so it'd take a week, maybe more, to fill the thing. By then I'd be out of plates." She tucked the leftovers into the fridge and turned. "Just stack them in the sink, I'll wash them later."

"I don't mind." He found the stopper for the sink and squirted in some soap. "Will you bring the pan over?"

"You really don't have to . . ." Vanessa broke off as Topher began to wash. He made a picture. There was something about a man doing dishes. "Thank you."

"Sure. Have any plans for the rest of the evening?"

"Not really. It's a weeknight, you know?" Not that she generally had plans on the weekend, either, but he didn't need to know that.

"Big day tomorrow?"

"No more than any Friday."

"Feel like a movie?"

Vanessa blinked. "Like out? I don't have any idea what's showing."

"You must have a DVD or two you particularly enjoy? Something to stream? Or we could go to my place, but I'm pretty sure Brian is in the middle of packing, so it might not be super conducive to watching something."

"Brian? You have a roommate?" How did she not know that?

Then again, why would she? Except he hadn't mentioned it and it seemed like something that would've come up at least once.

"Not really. He's a friend. Went through a bad breakup and needed a place to stay for a bit. Now, I guess he's feeling more settled and ready to move on." Topher shrugged. "In most ways it'll be nice to have my house back, but I didn't mind coming home to a hot dinner every now and then."

Vanessa chuckled. "I bet his girlfriend is missing out on those meals now, too. Jamie would sometimes have dinner put together—it's a nice thing to come home to."

"Boyfriend, but yeah."

Boyfriend. For Brian. "Oh. Well. Hmm."

"We've been friends since high school. I never thought his choices meant we should stop. And he doesn't seem to hold it against me that I talk to him about Jesus. I was hoping, honestly, that the breakup might push him a little closer. He's interested. I can see it. But he doesn't seem able to make the leap." Topher set the last dish in the drying rack and pulled the plug, letting the sudsy water escape down the drain.

Vanessa offered him a towel. "I get that. Think about it—the gay community has probably been the most accepting family he's had in his life. Even if you've been his friend, you've told him his lifestyle is sin, right?"

Topher nodded and folded the towel before setting it on the counter.

"How hard must it be to even consider walking away from that? How do you leave your family—everyone who has ever been one hundred percent in your corner—to follow someone who says those people, that family, is sin? It's a lot to give up."

"I never looked at it like that." Topher frowned. "You're right. It's a lot to ask. I still want it for him."

Vanessa reached for his hand and squeezed it. "Of course you do. And you're right to. But I think it's a lot like the rich young ruler who wouldn't give up his possessions to follow Jesus, even though that was the only way to get to the kingdom of Heaven—so just keep praying for him and being his friend."

"I can do that. Even if he decides he'd rather I didn't."

"I don't see how that's possible." Vanessa studied Topher's face. Why was she wasting time denying her attraction to him? Did she want to? "How about *The Princess Bride*?"

"Inconceivable!"

Vanessa grinned and pointed to where her DVDs were stored in neat rows under the TV. "Go ahead and find the disc, I'll toss some popcorn in the microwave."

"Sounds like a good deal." Topher crossed into the living area and squatted by the shelves.

Vanessa rummaged in her pantry for a bag of popcorn, sneaking glances over her shoulder at Topher. Maybe they weren't in a real relationship—but that didn't mean she couldn't try to make that change.

"I'm so glad you could make it out today. I'll confess I'm ever so slightly panicked." Claire pulled Vanessa into a tight hug before dragging her into the foyer. Peacock Hill never failed to steal Vanessa's breath. It was grand. Elegant. And Deidre's restoration had returned it to the full glory of the roaring twenties with modern conveniences tucked away.

"I didn't have any events so it was just a matter of getting someone to man the counter for a half day." She didn't do it a lot, but she had a handful of people she could call when push came to shove or she needed an extra hand. Thankfully, her first choice had been available and excited about a little extra cash.

"You brought an overnight bag?"

"Yep. So I'm yours for the weekend. I really think we can get you squared away for the ball. You're more prepared than you probably think."

"Now you sound like Deidre. She's so laid back sometimes I want to check to be sure she has a pulse."

Vanessa laughed.

"Anyway. What should we do first?"

She studied Claire. "Is the ball all you're stressing about? Honestly, you've handled a lot of events here already. This shouldn't be any more challenging."

"You'd think. Why don't you come down to my office?" Claire frowned. "That way we won't be interrupted."

Vanessa followed Claire to the basement stairs hidden behind a door under the grand staircase that led up to the second floor. In comparison, they were very simple stairs. Except that they'd been made from the same rich, dark wood and were twice as wide as a regular set of steps. They bypassed the small room dedicated as a business center of sorts for guests and stopped in front of a door marked "Office."

Claire pulled a ring of keys from her pocket. "I've started locking this when we have groups. Some of the teenagers, especially, seem to think it's fun to explore the basement. There's not much down here they can get into—so they try every doorknob."

Claire gestured for Vanessa to enter ahead of her. The room was small—big enough for an L-shaped desk and a couple of chairs. The wall behind a pair of computer monitors had been painted a sunny yellow, but otherwise there was no decoration.

"Isn't your apartment down here?"

"Yeah, mine and Deidre and Jeremiah's. You can get to mine through that door there," Claire nodded toward what Vanessa had assumed was a closet. "Or the main entrance down the hall a little bit from here. Dee's on the other side of the business center. We've always kept those doors locked though, so it hasn't been an issue."

Vanessa settled in one of the chairs across the desk from what was clearly Claire's work area. "Okay. Spill."

Claire closed the door and sighed. "You're a business woman. Do you ever get tired of having to do it all? It just never stops—there's my actual job of planning events, hunting down prospects for new business, and coordinating with groups once they're booked. I enjoy that. But then there's all the other stuff like haggling over insurance premiums and supplier costs and managing the finances. It's just . . . blech."

"Doesn't Deidre do some of it?" Vanessa had assumed—and wasn't that always a bad plan?—that the sisters shared the work on the business end of things.

"That was the original deal. But she hates it more than I do, so when push comes to shove, Dee's more likely to find something that needs fixing and go take care of that than to sit down and make sure the profit is getting split properly between all the vested parties."

Vanessa grinned. "Listen to you, vested parties."

Claire snorted. "Yeah, well. It's not how I pictured my life. I know our generation is supposed to strike out on our own and turn into entrepreneurs who do great things instead of settling down and slaving away for The Man. But honestly? There are a lot of days I think it wouldn't be so bad to clock a simple eight-hour day and collect a paycheck at the end of the month. No evenings. No weekends. No creeping expectations."

"I'm sorry. Have you talked to Deidre about this at all?" Shouldn't sisters be the best kind of business partners there were? Or maybe the sibling dynamics got involved and made it even messier.

"Tried. I don't think she's going to listen to anything and really hear it until she gets the nursery set up in their apartment.

Except I'm sure she'll find something else that's more pressing when that's done. She loves to tell me she trusts me to handle it. I appreciate her trust, I do, but I'm also getting tired of doing most of the work." Claire frowned. After a moment, she waved her hand like she was pushing it all aside. "Anyway. We aren't going to fix that today. Or this weekend. The ball. Let's focus on the ball."

"You're sure?"

Claire gave a brisk nod. "Yep. It's why you're here, right?"

It was. Although Vanessa valued the friendships she was beginning to make with the folks at Peacock Hill. Having Claire willing to share with her felt good. Like she belonged. All the ladies down here had a talent of doing just that. It wasn't something Vanessa had and she didn't take it for granted. "Did you get the sketches I emailed you?"

"Yeah." Claire opened a purple folder and spread out several papers. "You can do this with flowers? It seems ambitious."

Vanessa slid a drawing of a waist-height urn holding long stemmed grasses and flowers that fanned out like a peacock tail across the desk. "It's definitely ambitious. That doesn't mean it isn't doable. And with the crowd you're going to have for the ball, we need to push the envelope. They're mostly the bored rich, you know? Been there, done that, weren't all that impressed with the experience."

Claire swallowed visibly. "Are we going to be able to satisfy people like that? We don't have an enormous budget. As it is, I'm stretching beyond what Deidre wanted because it has such potential."

"I think that's smart. There's a rumor—and I can't say it's any more than that, so it may be completely unfounded—that the steering committee is looking for a permanent home for the ball rather than dealing with applications every year. It'd be a huge coup to snag that. But again, rumor." Except that her mother didn't usually mention things like this unless she had more than a little inside information. So, while technically it was a rumor, Vanessa was willing to put more stock in it than she would if it had come from any other source. "So I think it's worth our time to do what we can to knock everyone's socks off."

"All right. You know the people who are likely to come—where do we start?"

"Do you have the floorplans?"

Claire shuffled through the papers in the folder before sliding more drawings across the desk.

Vanessa studied the carefully drawn layout of the main floor of Peacock Hill and the garden areas close to the house before rubbing her hands together. "Okay. Let's get started."

16

Topher pulled into a parking spot in front of the little white church and frowned. What was he doing here?

When he'd texted Vanessa on Friday to thank her for dinner and a movie—and okay, fine, to see if she might want to do that again over the weekend—she'd mentioned she was coming down to Peacock Hill. It didn't quite compute with him that Claire needed any sort of help. The woman was a master of organization. He'd had a number of conversations with Sean about how he could easily hand off all aspects of the wedding day itself to Claire and not worry. Not that Sean would do that—he was entirely too hands-on and invested in the couples who used him to plan their weddings—but he could.

That was an enormous stamp of approval.

So the idea of Claire not being able to organize a ball for a couple hundred people? Pfft.

But Vanessa said Claire was nervous.

None of that explained why Topher was down here, though. Or why he'd reached out to Matt Patterson to wrangle an invitation of sorts to justify his visit.

He should turn around and go home. Well, drop off the

éclairs he'd thrown together first, and *then* go home. Hopefully before Vanessa saw him.

Someone tapped on the driver's side window.

Topher jolted and glanced over.

Matt grinned at him and jerked his head toward the church, his mouth moving.

Busted.

He pushed open the door and glanced over at the cooler holding the treats. They'd be fine in the car during the service. He hadn't planned on feeding the whole congregation, but it was tempting to throw them at Matt and head back to Richmond.

"I was wondering if you were going to join us or if you planned to sit in the car all morning. That seemed silly, given how early you had to hit the road to get here." Matt's voice rang with laughter.

Azure, his new wife, jabbed Matt in the ribs with her elbow. "Be nice. We're glad you came. Especially since I heard you were bringing dessert."

"Maybe I should just give you the box and head back. This was a dumb idea." Topher fumbled with the top of the cooler.

"Oh, stop." Azure shook her head. "At this point, you'll miss church if you go back. Don't be a chicken."

Topher stiffened. "I'm not—"

Matt snickered. "You kind of are at this point, unless you get out of the car."

"Are we twelve? I thought grownups were allowed to realize they'd made a tactical error and regroup."

"Listen to you. You've got it bad. Does she know?" Azure tugged the car door wider. "Or are you worried she'll figure it out?"

"We're just . . ." What were they? Friends? Kinda. Not really. They were maybe on the way to friendship. He found her attractive and interesting and wanted to spend more time getting to know her. He also had zero idea if she felt the same way. Did she simply need a date to the ball to keep her parents off her back? Was she humoring him so she didn't have to find someone else to go with? "It's tricky."

"Uh-huh. That's like saying it's complicated." Matt shook his head. "It's never as complicated as you think it is. Get out of the car, man. You don't want to miss the singing."

He really, really did. Topher wanted to miss the singing. And the preaching. And the singing that probably came afterward. And all of it. He wanted to miss all of it. Because this was a ridiculous miscalculation. "I think I'm going to—"

"Stop being a baby and get out of the car? Good." Matt jerked his head toward the church. "Come on."

Topher heaved out a breath and unhooked his seatbelt. "Fine. I'm not sure I realized you were this demanding."

Azure laughed and tugged Matt closer, hugging his arm. "You haven't seen anything. Flip side? He's usually right about stuff. It's annoying."

Matt kissed Azure's temple. "See? Listen to the lady. We hang out here much longer and my aunt's going to come find me. Then the third degree will start. And trust me, you don't want that."

"You really don't. And he won't back you up, at all. If Irene gets her teeth into this? Matt's going to be running for the hills. I won't be far behind him. You'll be on your own explaining why you're here to a woman who knows where all the bodies are buried and isn't afraid to remind you of it." Azure grinned up at Matt. "But she raised you, so she's not all bad."

"She loves you. She might not be sure what to do about it, but she loves you." Matt looked back at Topher. "You, on the other hand, she doesn't know. Yet. Come on. At least control the situation by showing up during the greeting time like a normal person."

"All right, all right." Topher gave the cooler a final glance before sliding out of the car. He hit the lock button and tucked his hands in his pockets. "Next time I call you looking for an excuse to visit, remind me that it's a bad idea."

"WHAT BROUGHT YOU DOWN HERE TODAY?" Deidre passed Topher the salad.

Conversation around the long table in the dining room at Peacock Hill seemed to stall. He could feel everyone's eyes on him. Topher fumbled with the salad tongs. "Uh . . ."

"I'm actually really glad you're here." Topher pictured Claire throwing him a life buoy with her words. Her smile suggested she knew he owed her. "Vanessa and I could use your thoughts on the catering bids I have for this ball we're hosting at the start of November."

"It sounds so ridiculous and old fashioned." Danny pulled a face and adopted a snooty accent. "We're having a baaaallll, dahling. What were you thinking, Dee? I thought you were all about Christian events."

"We are." Deidre frowned and poked at her food. "And weddings. I don't think hosting one charity ball is going to undermine our mission here."

"Charity being one of the keywords." Claire's tone lowered the temperature in the room by about half.

Topher picked up his water. He'd been told there was tension between Claire and Danny, but this was the first time he'd seen it.

"The money raised is going to support some of the residential facilities for children in the state where kids end up for various reasons when they can't stay with family and aren't placed or can't remain in more traditional foster homes." Claire set down her fork and glared across the table at Danny. "Seems to me Jesus said a word or two about widows and orphans, so an event to help the less fortunate fits right in with being a Christian event center."

Danny held up his hands like he was fending off an attack. "Seems like the pricey ticket could be used for those donations and people could skip the ball is all I'm saying. Then there wouldn't have to be a raffle on top of everything."

"Actually," Topher cleared his throat as attention swung back to him, "I was doing a little research since I'm coming, and I like to know what I'm attending. The ticket price does primarily go to the designated charity. The foundation website has a break-down and their annual report from last year. They do a lot of good. And the board has a lot of names I recognize from other, more explicitly Christian events. So maybe the foundation isn't restricted to believers, but it's full of them."

Vanessa smiled at him and mouthed, "Thank you."

Topher looked down at his food and let the warm glow spread through him. He'd been taken aback by the price of the tickets—and Vanessa had been adamant that she was covering both of them since she'd been the one to invite him. He could have afforded his. And maybe even hers if he'd rearranged his budget. But she'd acted like it was no big deal to drop close to five grand on one night's entertainment. Did her shop do that well? It was hard to picture. Maybe she saved all year so she could go? There were questions, and he wasn't sure how to get the answers.

Or if he was entitled to them.

He tried to hang back from the rest of the lunch conversa-tion, responding only when someone went out of the way to draw him in. The group at Peacock Hill was close—like a family —it left him with a little ache under his breastbone.

"Penny for your thoughts?" Vanessa slid into the seat beside him.

Topher hadn't noticed it was empty. "I wasn't planning to go home for Christmas this year."

She let out a short laugh. "Not at all what I would have guessed if you'd given me a hundred chances. Go on."

"I was thinking about the gang here—they're like a family. It made me miss mine and regret, just a little, not going home for Christmas."

"Could you go home if you wanted?"

That was the big question. It was one of the shop's busiest times. People liked their special order desserts for big parties and family gatherings. "I don't know. My staff could absolutely handle the craziness of special and last minute orders. I've been mulling what I should do, if anything, about how unnecessary I feel there most days. But just because they can handle it, I'm not sure it's fair to ask them to. I mean Christmas, right? Some of them will want vacation too."

"Do you close at all?"

"Yeah. And I could expand those dates a little. Give us all more of a break. Mom and Dad are in Florida, so it's not like I have to go far to get home. I could go for a couple of days, close everything. It's something to think about. Do you go home for Christmas?"

Vanessa wrinkled her nose. "You ask like you think I have a choice. Of course I do. You've met my mother."

"I liked your mom."

She sighed. "Yeah, I do too. Love her, even. But sometimes . . . maybe it's a mother daughter thing."

"No, I get it. Some parents have a harder time letting their kids be adults than others. Especially, I think . . ." he trailed off.

Was he overstepping if he mentioned her brother? It's just an observation. He had no real facts to back anything up.

"Especially?"

"When one of their kids has gone a direction they don't like and they weren't able to help them get back on track." He winced. "It's just an idea."

"Jamie." Vanessa nodded. "Yeah, I can see that. I left home about the time he completely cut us out of his life. And Mom took a dive off the deep end. I hadn't thought about it like that. Maybe now that he's home, she'll lighten up."

"Maybe." He glanced at the empty room and frowned. "Where'd everyone go?"

Vanessa laughed. "You really zoned out. They're in the kitchen doing dishes and then there's talk of ultimate Frisbee up on the big lawn above the lion fountain."

It was a pretty space. He'd only seen it done up for weddings, but it would make a good Frisbee ground as well. "I didn't bring sneakers."

"Neither did I. I'll admit that was on purpose if you promise not to tell anyone. Claire mentioned the possibility when we were talking about me coming down. I hate Frisbee."

"How can you hate Frisbee?"

"I inevitably break a nail. And yes, I know how that sounds. I may keep them short for work, but that doesn't mean I want them wrecked by a flying plastic disc."

Topher snickered. "If it's hitting your fingernails, I'm pretty sure you're doing it wrong."

Vanessa rolled her eyes. "Thanks ever so much. Anyway, Claire and I wanted to talk to you about desserts for the ball and get your thoughts. All of the catering proposals have a lot of detail on the finger food, but dessert always seems like an afterthought. Come down and see?"

"Sure." He pushed back from the table and stood. "Lead the way."

Topher had never spent a lot of time inside Peacock Hill. The weddings he'd worked on had usually entailed an outdoor reception. He couldn't quite help craning his neck to catch details as they passed through the foyer, beyond the sweeping grandeur of the staircase and stained glass window on the first landing, to a door that blended seamlessly with the wood paneling of the back hall. He caught a glimpse of a marble fire-place with a colorful mural above it before nearly running into Vanessa.

"Do you need a tour?"

He shrugged and hoped the heat crawling up his neck wasn't translating into the dark red flush that usually accompanied it. "I don't do a lot inside when I'm here."

"I can get Claire to show you around after if you want?"

"Maybe she'd let me wander. I don't need the history or stories, but I wouldn't mind poking around."

"You're such a guy." Vanessa yanked open the door and led Topher downstairs to the basement.

"Guilty." He grinned and took in the more modern, func-tional space. The little business center with simple desks and streamlined computers at each workstation, the Berber carpet designed to repel dirt and wear. "They did a nice job down here."

Vanessa nodded before knocking on the door marked "Office."

"Come on in."

"She beat us down. How'd we miss her?" Topher hadn't seen Claire walk by. Then again, he'd been focused on Vanessa—he might not have noticed an earthquake.

"Elevator, probably. That access is closer to the kitchen and we probably wouldn't have seen her the way we were angled in the dining room." Vanessa pushed open the door and gestured for Topher to go in. "Have a seat."

"I'm so glad you ended up down here today. Vanessa was going to take copies of these bids home and see if you'd look at them this week, but I'm getting nervous. If we need to find additional catering, we're about five weeks out. I know that's cutting it close." Claire pushed a file across the desk.

Topher sat and drew the papers closer. The bids were pretty standard—nothing overly creative. Or interesting, if they were asking his opinion. He drew his eyebrows together and studied them in light of the ticket price. Did people really not want actual food?

"What?" Vanessa put her hand on his shoulder.

Everything in him stilled even as his heart took off. "I guess I don't understand why it's not a plated meal."

"It used to be. The focus really is on the dancing and the raffle now. So it's finger food and dessert. Everyone knows to eat dinner beforehand. It's why they moved the start time to eight. I've never bothered with a meal ahead of time and still haven't left hungry." Vanessa shrugged.

"Okay." He flipped a page and zeroed in on the dessert listing and quantities. "They're expecting everyone to fill up before they come. And then use the appetizers to handle any other hunger. Throw in the usual 'oh, I couldn't possibly, I'm on a diet' that you'll get from most of the women at something like this— especially if they're in a more form-fitting gown? This is probably fine."

Claire chuckled. "I hadn't thought about the vanity factor. You wouldn't do anything different?"

"I don't know if I'd say that." Topher closed the folder and tapped it. "I think I'd add some kind of centerpiece dessert. Being me, I'd go with a cake. The mini bakery items—éclairs, cream puffs, custard tarts, pies—those are great finger foods and a woman can choose one, maybe two, and feel like she's had dessert. If that's all there is though? A guy's going to load up a plate, then go home and have a Ho Ho."

"A Ho Ho? There's no way you eat Ho Hos." Vanessa's eyes danced with mirth.

"Sure I do, what's not to love? Thin chocolate wrapped around cake rolled up with cream in the middle? Yum. But okay, maybe they'll skew Ding Dong."

Claire laughed. "I get the picture. They won't be satisfied."

"Exactly. So, if it was me, I'd tack on a cake that serves maybe half or three-quarters of your expected attendance. That way you don't end up swimming in leftover cake, but you have a better, more filling option for the people who didn't go out to eat ahead of time but are looking for a more substantial dessert." Topher shrugged. "Of course that means you need at least two extra servers to cut slices and maybe pass a tray, plus forks."

"Could you do it?"

"Pass cake slices?"

Vanessa poked him. "The cake. Bake the cake."

He sorted through the schedule of events he'd already contracted and nodded. "Yeah, I could do that. I'll even do it at cost."

"Seriously?" Claire brightened. "I didn't want to ask, but that'd be a huge help. Anything we add is coming out of our profit."

"And you bid low to get the gig. Vanessa mentioned it. Smart move, by the way." Topher drummed his fingers on his leg. "I'll send you some sketches and estimates this week, by say Wednesday? Can the caterer's servers handle the serving and passing plus plates and forks?"

"I'll check. I can't see why not. Thanks, Topher." Claire stood. "You two joining us for Frisbee?"

Vanessa shook her head. "I don't have the right shoes."

"Uh-huh. Topher?"

"Not today. I should get home. Do you mind if I poke around the house first though?"

Claire's eyebrows lifted. "Haven't you had the tour?"

"Nope. I'm usually outside in a tent."

"Huh. Sure, go nuts. I think all the upstairs rooms are unlocked since they're empty this weekend. We've got a small group checking in tomorrow, so if you see something that doesn't look right, would you let me know before you leave?"

"Sure. Thanks." He glanced at Vanessa. "Feel like taking the non-tour with me?"

He held Vanessa's gaze and could practically hear her weighing pros and cons before she managed a slow nod. "Yeah, okay."

Topher caught Claire's smirk and shrugged. He didn't care if people knew he was interested in Vanessa. Vanessa might. But that was her problem. "I hear there's an elevator. Any problem with us starting at the top and working our way back down?"

"Nope. It's just out in the hall—looks like a closet. Have fun. And seriously, Topher, thanks again."

Topher stepped into the basement hallway. Finding the elevator access was easy enough. Since the car was there, the doors opened as soon as he hit the button. "Guess you're right, she took the elevator down."

Vanessa stepped in, her fingers twisted into a knot in front of her. She stayed that way—distant and withdrawn, through most of the tour. Even the quick trip up into one of the side towers at the front of the building didn't relax her.

Back in the foyer, Topher fought a frown. He'd hoped for a few minutes alone with Vanessa—and he'd gotten them—but the easy camaraderie they'd shared before had disappeared. "Well. I guess I'll get going. It was good to see you."

"Why did you come down today, Topher?" Vanessa stood

stiff, arms crossed, her forehead creased in what looked like the beginning of a scowl.

Had they lost all the ground they'd gained? Topher closed the distance between them. Maybe it was time to lay some cards on the table. He pressed the faintest whisper of a kiss to the furrow between her brows. "I wanted to see you."

17

Vanessa scowled at the invoice from her supplier. The totals were fine. A little better than fine, in fact. So what was her problem?

She huffed out a breath and tossed the paper aside.

Topher.

Topher was the problem.

He wanted to see her? What did that even mean?

Obviously, it meant he'd wanted to see her. But why? He hadn't gone out of his way to have any particularly meaningful conversation. So it wasn't that he wanted to see her in order to discuss whatever was on his mind.

She should just ask him.

Vanessa reached for her cell then set it back down as the bell in the front of her shop rang. "Coming."

Wiping her hands on her apron, she crossed through the doorway into the front and squealed. "Jamie!"

"Hey, Ness." He grinned and held out a white paper sack. "Brought you some coffee almond."

"Ice cream? Seriously?" Vanessa snatched the bag and peeked into it. Bouncing on the balls of her feet she grinned across the counter at him. "You're the best big brother ever. Come on back. Did you get yourself some?"

"I figured I'd just steal a bite of yours."

"Nuh-uh." She clutched the bag to her chest. "Mine."

"Greedy." He chuckled as he followed her to the back room and settled on one of the stools at her worktable. "I guess it's good I ate mine in the car."

"Ha. See?" Vanessa plopped on the other stool and dug into the bag from her favorite ice cream shop, bringing out the paper cup of ice cream. She popped off the lid and dipped the plastic spoon in, closing her eyes as she took the first bite. "Mmm. No one makes it better."

"So you've always said. I will admit their mint chip was decent."

"Anyone can do mint chip."

"Untrue. If it isn't green, it's not going to be as good."

She snickered and spooned up another bite. "There's no way food coloring makes something taste better."

Jamie shrugged. "You can laugh, but it's true. I've done extensive testing. The white mint chips are never as good."

Vanessa shook her head and continued to eat as she studied her brother. He looked good. Better than he had when he'd shown up at her door at the start of September, that was for sure. "So. How's life as a suit?"

He winced. "Don't call me that."

"Tell me you don't wear one to the office."

"Clothing choices don't necessarily indicate personality. Or the enjoyment of the job."

Uh oh. "You don't like it?"

"Actually, I do. More than I imagined was possible. Dad—either he's mellowed some or I seriously misunderstood the job he was offering me before I left."

Vanessa considered, tapping her spoon on the edge of the

cup. "Maybe a little of both. Although I'm not sure I'd go as far as calling Dad mellow."

"Didn't say he was mellow. I said he was *mellower*. Those last two letters matter."

She nodded. Mellower was definite. Then again, it wouldn't have taken much. "In that case, Mom's mellowed some as well."

"I'll take your word for it. She sends me the phone number of no fewer than three eligible young women each week."

"Yikes."

"Tell me." Jamie dipped his finger in her ice cream, scooping out a chocolate covered almond and popping it in his mouth before she could object. "Now that you're practically engaged, Mom says she can focus her efforts on me."

Vanessa choked on her ice cream.

Jamie's eyes narrowed. "As you can imagine, I was surprised to find out about your impending nuptials from Mom. Who's the lucky guy?"

"There isn't one."

"Uh-huh. Not what Mom says. Even Dad seems to be of the opinion that you're in a serious relationship with the guy you're bringing to the Founder's Ball?"

"Are you coming?"

He wagged a finger at her. "Don't try to change the subject."

"Topher. I'm going with Topher. But we're not engaged. We're not even dating. Not for real. We went to dinner at Mom and Dad's and they liked him and Mom got the bit between her teeth. It seemed easier to play along. Topher said he was fine with the ball, but that if we were going to be successful at convincing Mom and Dad we were a couple we should go out a few times." Vanessa shrugged. "So we did."

"That's it?"

That should be it. It was supposed to be all there was.

Vanessa frowned. "He showed up at Peacock Hill on Sunday afternoon."

"What were you doing there?" Jamie reached across the table and slid her ice cream cup in front of him. He scooped up a big bite.

"Planning flowers—and a bit more—for the ball. Claire's nervous. I still don't get that, to be honest. She's handled events way more complicated, but this one is throwing her. There's something going on with her, but I've only pried out a little."

"Focus, Nessa. Topher. What did he say when you asked why he was there?"

She drew her eyebrows together. "What makes you think I asked why he was there?"

"Didn't you?"

"Yes."

Jamie simply smiled.

"Fine. He said he wanted to see me. But why? He didn't have any particular question to ask or anything like that, so what did he want to see me about?"

Jamie's snicker morphed into a chortle and then a full-bellied laugh.

She waited several minutes then crossed her arms. She could feel the scowl working its way across her features but had no ability to stop it. "So glad I amuse you."

"Vanessa." He paused and gasped for breath. "Are you really this dense?"

"I'm not den—"

"He wanted to see you. Because for all your protestations that it's a ruse to keep Mom off your back, Topher clearly wants this relationship to be real. He likes you."

"Likes . . . No way."

"Seriously. When was the last time you went out on a date?"

Vanessa gestured to the shop. "I'm a little busy."

"Oh, sure, I can tell. It's crazy in here."

Fine. Maybe things were a little—or a lot—slower than she'd prefer right now. But that wasn't always the case. She made ends meet. Even squirreled away a little profit for a rainy day, so it wasn't as if she was living hand to mouth. "This is always a slow time of year. It'll pick up again in another two weeks when high schools have Homecoming. I do a brisk corsage and boutonniere business for that. Then table arrangements for Thanksgiving and Christmas, plus housewarming. Add in all the usual 'I messed up' or congratulations flowers and I'm doing okay."

"I wasn't trying to insult your business." Jamie pushed the empty ice cream container back to the middle of the table. "I was pointing out that you might be a little out of touch when it comes to understanding the male of the species."

"I've never understood the male of the species," Vanessa muttered. She grabbed the container and pressed the lid back on before dropping it back in the paper sack.

"Exactly. So take it from me—I have firsthand knowledge of the guy, you recall—he likes you and is hoping to turn this fake relationship into something real."

Her heart gave a funny little skip. "I'm not sure how to do that."

"Just be you, Ness. I'm guessing that's who he's half in love with anyway."

She leaned away from the table. Love? That was . . . she'd take like. He liked her. Love was a ridiculous notion.

"Don't look so scared. Love doesn't hurt. Not when you're in it, at least."

"Right. But what about when it ends?"

"WHAT ARE WE LOOKING AT?" Vanessa glanced over at Topher as

he unlocked the door to a storefront in a busy strip of shops on the other side of the city. She was rarely over this way—everything she needed could be found in her little pocket of Richmond.

"Come see." He tugged open the door and held it for her. When she stepped through, he fumbled on the wall for light switches and, as the overheads hummed to life, flipped the top lock. "Hmm."

Round café tables with old-timey ice cream parlor type chairs were pushed against the wall leaving the majority of the space empty. At the far end was a long glass display case. Behind that was a dark doorway. "Café?"

"Used to be. Some sort of coffee over ice cream thing—there's an Italian name for it. But that's all they sold. As much as people liked it, it wasn't enough to keep them afloat. I guess they wouldn't sell the ice cream separately. It was their concoction or nothing."

"That's a bit of a hard line." Vanessa crossed the room to peer into the display case. The bottom was clearly a freezer designed for holding buckets of ice cream. She pointed to the doorway. "There's a kitchen?"

"So I'm told. Let's check it out." Topher felt around the corner and, after a moment, the lights in there flashed on.

"I'm still not sure why we're looking at an old café on a Friday night." When he'd called to see if she wanted to do something, she hadn't been able to say no. He'd kept to himself all week—probably busy at his bakery or with outside events. That was reasonable. Even expected. But she'd missed him.

It was inexplicable.

Unless you were her brother. Jamie had taken to sending random little texts teasing her about Topher.

Topher paused in the act of running his hand along a stainless steel counter and cocked his head to the side. "I've been thinking of opening a second location. They don't need me on anything resembling a daily basis at the bakery. I do all the wedding cakes and if we get a special event cake, I do that, but the day-to-day stuff? That's been out of my hands since the wedding cakes started taking off."

"And you miss it?" Why not just be more involved? "Couldn't you, I don't know, remind everyone who's in charge?"

He threw his head back and laughed. "I could, sure. I don't want to. I love that they've got it under control and I don't have to get up at four in the morning if I don't want to. I enjoy the business side of things a lot. Two stores would give me more of that to handle. And sure, when we were getting started, I'd probably have to pitch in more, which is fine. But within a year I imagine I could have a solid staff handling things every bit as well as the other shop. And a second location is going to increase the cake business, too."

Vanessa wrinkled her nose. "The business side of things is a necessary evil in my mind. I love having my own flower shop, but primarily because it means I get to play with flowers all day, every day. The realization that I'm going to have to officially take on some help in the spring if it looks like I've got another wedding season like this last one makes me sad. Not only because of the extra paperwork it'll involve."

"I get that. I started out that way." Topher slid his arm around her shoulder but continued to study the kitchen space. He rubbed her shoulder. "Sometimes feelings change."

Vanessa's breath caught in her lungs. She glanced over at him, but he was still focused on the tiny commercial kitchen. Feelings could change. Did change. "Yeah, they do."

One corner of his mouth poked up, and he slowly turned his head so he was looking at her. He leaned in slowly and brushed his lips across hers.

When Topher began to step back, Vanessa turned and

wrapped both arms around his neck. She twined her fingers through his hair and drew his head closer. She had a moment to grin at the surprise on his face before she brought their lips back together.

If something was worth doing, it was worth doing right.

Kissing Topher was definitely worth doing.

18

Topher eased out of the kiss and pressed his lips to Vanessa's forehead before wrapping his arms around her tighter and resting his cheek on the top of her head. His heart thundered in his chest, and every nerve ending was hyper-aware of his contact with her body.

She sighed and burrowed closer.

Topher chuckled and squeezed before loosening his arms and stepping back. "What do you think of the kitchen?"

Vanessa blinked. "The kitchen?"

He nodded.

She lifted a shoulder. "It seems kitcheny."

He laughed and tapped the tip of her nose with his finger. "It does at that. As much as it pains me though, I'm not sure it's big enough as it is for how I'd want to use it. I'll have to call my architect and see if he has time to come take a look so he could get me an idea of what it would take to expand. I don't need as much space out front, so that's not a problem, but their asking price here is already on the top end of what I want to pay."

"Okay."

Topher reached out and wove his fingers through hers. "Dinner?"

"I ate before you called. Are we really not going to talk about that kiss?" She tugged on her hand.

He held tighter and drew her close. "Do we need to?"

"I think so."

She sounded so prim, Topher had to fight a smile. "Okay. You start."

Vanessa opened her mouth then snapped it shut and looked away. "You're making fun of me."

"I'm not." He waited until she looked at him again. "Promise. I've wanted to kiss you for a lot longer than I've been willing to admit. Even to myself. Now that I have? I'd like to do it again."

Pink tinged her cheeks and her lips curved. "Oh."

"That said, if you're feeling even half of what I am, I think maybe food's a better idea. Some place with a lot more people around. You already ate, so dessert?" He'd never considered himself someone who struggled with self control. In fact, he'd been a little . . . smug was probably the word, when confronted with friends who wrestled with the idea of staying celibate until marriage. He'd always thought—and said—it was something he'd made up his mind to do, so it'd never be a problem.

One kiss with Vanessa, well, two, depending on how technical he wanted to get, and he understood a whole lot more clearly.

"I like ice cream."

"Who doesn't?" Topher grinned and tugged her hand. "Let's see if we can find some nearby."

"You have an architect?"

Topher frowned as he unlocked the door and pushed it open for Vanessa to exit. He double-checked that the lights were off before closing up and pocketing the key. "What?"

"You said you'd talk to your architect. Like people talk about,

I don't know, their lawyer or housekeeper or something." She shrugged.

"Ah. I guess I could have said I'd talk to the architect I've used in the past who I'm friendlyish with, but that seemed like a mouthful."

Vanessa snorted. "You're making fun again."

"A little. I also have several contacts in real estate, which is how I come to have a key to an empty store front on a Friday night. One of them was willing to trust me with it, because she knows I'd rather check it out on my own without her blathering about square footage and the perks of the surrounding retail area." Did he have to mention that he and said real estate agent had dated a few times? She was in a serious relationship now and already talking to Topher about wedding cakes, despite not technically having a ring on her finger quite yet. He'd let it go unless Vanessa brought it up.

"I wondered." She slanted a look up at him. "Are we walking in search of ice cream? Driving? Looking something up on a phone so we don't wander aimlessly?"

"Let's do that last one." He slid his phone out of his back pocket and tapped the screen. After a moment he chuckled. "*Affogato*."

"Never heard of it."

"You and most of the area, apparently. That's what they used to sell here—the coffee and, oh my bad, espresso not coffee. With gelato."

"I've never been a huge fan of gelato. Give me ice cream any day."

Topher laughed and continued to scroll. There were a couple of nearby choices. None within walking distance though. "Looks like we'll have to drive."

"Okay."

Topher opened the car door for Vanessa and scooted around

to his side. Maybe he could talk her into someplace she could get a milkshake and he could get dinner. He was starving. And if his mouth was occupied with a thick, juicy burger, maybe he wouldn't be quite so focused on figuring out when he could kiss Vanessa again.

Who was he kidding? One of the first requirements for a good baker was the ability to multitask.

And Topher was a good baker.

"I'm glad it worked out for us to have lunch after the service today." Sean leaned back in his chair at the square table in a popular Mexican chain restaurant and sighed. "Feels like our weekends have been overwhelming lately."

Larissa laughed. "That's because we've been seeing family. Your family terrifies me. My family terrifies you."

"Terrifies is a bit harsh."

Topher chuckled. "Family can be tricky."

"Tell me." Vanessa frowned at Topher. "I haven't met yours."

Larissa's eyebrows lifted. "Why would you?"

Pink flooded Vanessa's face and she reached for her water.

"I've met hers." Topher shrugged. "Seems reasonable, I guess?"

"But the two of you . . . you're always insisting there's nothing going on." Larissa switched her attention between them. "I knew it!"

"Larissa . . ." Sean reached for her hand.

"No. It's okay. It's newish." Vanessa glanced at Topher.

Newish worked. They'd started their fake relationship a couple of weeks ago, but Topher imagined that probably didn't count. Friday, though, Friday counted.

"Define newish."

Topher cocked his head and studied Sean. "Really?"

"Hey, some of us are curious. Especially given previous conversations that I imagine you'd rather we not get into."

He would, in fact, rather they not be gotten into. Or even mentioned. He could feel Vanessa's curiosity and it was inevitable that he'd end up having to explain that he'd complained about her to Sean. More than once. That was unlikely to go over well. "Two days."

"Friday? You told me you were looking at a new retail space on Friday and that's why you couldn't hang out." Sean shook his head. "You were that embarrassed about dating Vanessa you lied to me?"

"I didn't lie. We looked at a retail space." Topher covered Vanessa's hand with his. "Then we had dinner."

"A milkshake." Vanessa pointed at Topher. "I only had a milkshake."

"It's true." Topher squeezed her hand.

Larissa reached for a chip and dunked it in the dregs of the salsa. "That's not a very good first date."

Sean eyed Larissa. "Our first date was related to planning your wedding to someone else. I'm pretty sure we don't have any room to talk."

"None of that counts." Larissa dropped the chip, uneaten, on her plate. "I've got to stop eating. I'm ready to burst. But they're right in front of me and they're so yummy."

Vanessa reached into the middle of the table and started stacking the dishes. "Here. This'll help."

"Maybe." Larissa chewed on her lip before helping to stack plates, making sure to cover the dregs of the chips in the basket. "I still know they're there though."

Vanessa chuckled.

Topher pushed his chair back from the table. "Should we just go? Then the temptation is over."

Larissa reached behind her and unhooked her purse from the back of her chair. "That's not a bad idea. I have a ton of papers to grade before tomorrow. When I started back teaching, I had all these plans that I was going to keep work at work—or at least not drag it home on the weekends. I didn't even make it through the first quarter."

"Yet another reason I never seriously considered teaching as a career. Flowers don't follow me home."

"Don't they?" Topher cocked his head to the side and studied Vanessa. "Weren't you the one telling me you could only swing lunch after church because you had to get back and deal with the paperwork you keep putting off?"

"That's different." Vanessa crossed her arms.

"Yeah, not so much." Larissa grinned. "But I won't judge if you don't."

"It's harder not to work on Sunday than it should be. And coming out to lunch, for that matter, means we're contributing to others needing to work." Vanessa frowned. "Are we breaking a commandment? I mean seriously, the Bible's pretty clear."

"Eating out?" Topher shook his head. "For that I'm going to say no. The servers and so forth would be here working regardless of whether or not we came. Even if every single Christian in Richmond stopped eating out after church, there are plenty of people who aren't believers who help keep them open. If no one can work on Sunday, then how does anyone at church get away with it?"

Sean laughed. "That's one way to look at it, isn't it? I don't think the pastor is breaking a commandment by preaching on Sunday. But I also kind of think it's one of those areas where people need to individually let the Holy Spirit work in their lives. If you're feeling convicted, then maybe you need to step back and pray about what you should be doing."

Larissa nodded. "I am. I do. I knew I should do the grading

yesterday, but I put it off, so some of my problem is the guilt from having put something off when I had the time to do it."

Vanessa groaned and raised her hand. "Also guilty. Which doesn't change what I need to do today, but I can work on doing better going forward."

Sean glanced at Topher. "Since the women are busy, feel like hanging out for a bit?"

Topher shrugged. He didn't have anything planned for the day. He'd been hoping to talk Vanessa into a walk somewhere, or maybe a drive out to Peacock Hill. It wasn't that far, and the gang there was usually happy to have drop-ins. But if she was working. "Sure, why not?"

"THAT DIDN'T TAKE AS LONG as I figured it would." Sean's eyes danced with laughter as he stepped back to let Topher into his apartment.

Topher tucked his hands in his pockets. "Yeah, well, we haven't been dating long, so it's not as if we're getting caught up in long kisses goodbye."

"Uh-huh." Sean shut the door. "But you want to."

"Goes without saying, doesn't it?"

Sean grinned. "Probably. Although I have fond memories of you pulling me aside and remarking on how awful she was. Those'll be good to drag out at your rehearsal dinner. You're going to let me plan your wedding, right?"

"Why didn't I realize before now that you were a comedian? Oh, right, because you're not funny."

"Come on, you have to admit it's hilarious."

"Sure. As long as you find it just as funny that you were in the act of helping Larissa walk down the aisle to someone else when you fell in love with her."

Sean shrugged. "It's almost amusing now. At least Tom finally gave up and moved out of the area. That's helped her. A lot. In fact . . ."

Topher waited, but Sean didn't continue. "In fact what?"

"That's kind of why I was hoping you'd be free to hang out today." Sean pointed to the sofa. "Take a seat. I'll be right back."

Okay. Maybe Sean was finally losing his mind. It was inevitable. Anyone who could juggle as many details for all the different events—especially the weddings—like Sean did was bound to crack.

Topher settled back on the couch and propped his feet on the big square ottoman that, apparently, also served as a coffee table. At least if the magazines and takeout cups on it were any indication. He leaned forward and pushed them around, chuckling.

"What's funny?" Sean sat beside Topher and flipped open his laptop.

"It's not every guy who has more bridal than video game magazines in their living room."

"Professional hazard." Sean tapped on his keyboard before angling the screen so Topher could see. "I need help making a decision."

Topher looked over and his eyebrows shot up. "Wow. Okay."

"Is it too soon? I've talked myself in and out of the timing so many times I don't know what I'm doing. What I do know is that I love Larissa. I can't imagine my life without her in it, and I want to get started on that life together as soon as she'll let us." Sean dragged a hand through his hair. "If she'd do it tomorrow, I'd drag her out to this historic home in Culpeper that does elopements."

"Kinda bad for business if the wedding planner elopes." Topher reached for the laptop and settled it on his lap so he could study the four engagement rings currently displayed on the webpage. "These are all custom?"

"Semi. You buy the diamond and the setting separately—but they have recommendations of what works with what. I've had a lot of brides with rings from these guys—the grooms all go on and on about what a great shopping experience it was, so I figured it was better than some chain store at the mall. Plus no chance of someone seeing what I'm doing and word getting out."

Topher nodded. The mall chain was a definite no, but there were some nice mom and pop jewelry stores downtown. Still, referrals counted, and these looked nice on the monitor. "You sure you want to drop this much cash without having touched it?"

Sean shrugged. "I don't know. I know I don't want to go to the mall."

Topher laughed and opened a new tab on the browser. After a quick search, he angled the laptop for Sean to see. "What about looking here? I imagine they'd keep things quiet if you mentioned you'd like them to."

"They have estate jewelry too. Hmm." Sean pulled the computer onto his lap and clicked.

Topher fought the urge to chuckle at Sean's expression—so serious. And okay, sure, buying an engagement ring was a big deal, but Sean looked like he thought the fate of the world rested on making the right decision.

"All right. Let's go."

"Now?"

Sean nodded and set the laptop on the ottoman. "They close in two hours. And they have a vintage piece I really need to see."

"Better than the online store?"

"Maybe." Sean frowned. "Okay, probably. No gloating."

Topher pushed to his feet and held up his hand like he was taking an oath. "No gloating. At least where you can see it."

Sean punched Topher's arm.

"Just for that, I'm driving."

"You say that like it's punishment, but man, I don't care. If you know how to get there, then you should be driving anyway. Let me go grab my checkbook."

"Your checkbook? Okay, Grandma."

"Yeah, yeah. I keep a low limit on my cards and I don't want to max anything out. I have the money in the bank, so yes. Checkbook."

Topher shrugged. If people still took checks that was their business. He didn't. And he had no plans to start. Cash or credit. His employees were on his case to add on the various phone payment deals, but his equipment was older and wasn't set up for contactless payment. He was keeping an eye on it—if it looked like he was losing business because he didn't accept those options, he'd take the plunge. But for now, cash and credit was plenty.

"You ready?"

"Yeah, come on. Let's go get you a ring."

19

Vanessa slit the top of the box with her scissors and set them aside. It was well past closing, but there was too much to do to prepare for the Founder's Ball in . . . wow, twenty-six days, and not all of them were work days. Three were Sundays, and she was going to do better about not working on Sundays. Two of the Saturdays were busy with previously booked events—a fiftieth anniversary party and a baby shower. Those events would need at least two days of prep, which left her what? Sixteen days.

How was she supposed to prep arrangements for an event like the Founder's Ball in sixteen days?

Vanessa drew in a deep breath and tried to hold it, but her hammering heart made it hard. She tried again. Then a third time. And now she was practically hyperventilating. She lowered her head to her knees and focused on letting out each breath she took in. There wasn't time for this.

There wasn't time for anything.

Her cell started ringing.

Vanessa patted the table until her fingers closed around it. "Hello?"

"Why aren't you home? It's nearly eight."

"Jamie?"

"Got it in one. It was a nasty drive down—who knew traffic on 95 was awful on Tuesdays?"

"Everyone who lives in the area? Traffic is bad on any day that ends in y. Wait—you're here?"

"Ha. That's a good one. A day that ends in y. Yeah, I've been knocking on your door for the last ten minutes. Where are you? Hot date?"

"Only if unpacking special order urns is a hot date. I'm downstairs. Come down to the back door, I'll let you in."

"Got any food down there?"

Vanessa sighed. Dinner wasn't a terrible idea. "No. But I can make a call. Potstickers?"

"Oh, yeah. You make the call, I'll pay."

There was a rap on the back door. Vanessa laughed and ended the call. Her brother was exactly the antidote to panic that she needed. She strode to the back door and wrenched it open. "Hey."

"Hey yourself." He ambled in and slung an arm over her shoulder. "That's . . . a lot of boxes."

Vanessa turned slightly, closed and relocked the door, then surveyed the delivery that had come just before closing. The boxes were stacked in every available space. It was going to be cramped working in here until the ball. Maybe she should have had everything shipped directly to Peacock Hill, but then she wouldn't have been able to check for damage as easily. If something was broken, or the wrong item, she needed to fix it sooner rather than later. "Yeah. Founder's Ball."

"Nice." Jamie squeezed her shoulders before releasing her. "You call for the food yet?"

"No. I'll do it now." She studied her brother as he moved around her workroom. He could still use another five, maybe ten pounds, but the bespoke suit, complete with cufflinks winking at his wrists, fit him better than anything she'd seen him in lately. "You look good, Jamie."

"Feel good. I'm not sure why I gave Mom and Dad such a hard time about this job. It's like I was born for it."

Vanessa snorted. He had been. Surely he saw that. She swiped open the app for the Chinese place a block down and tapped her standard order twice. "Done. It'll be about fifteen."

"Great. I'll pay when they come."

She held up her phone. "App. Sorry."

"Next time. You sure you can afford it?"

"Please. It's like fifteen bucks. I have the ball flowers, remember?"

"Sure. But have they paid you yet?"

Claire had offered. Vanessa turned her down. Committees—particularly those chaired by people who had no idea how much was in their checking account at any point in time—were notoriously slow to pay. They'd get around to giving Claire the venue deposit, and that would be enough that Claire could turn around and get Vanessa the first half of the flower money, but until then she could make it work. "You know what society events are like."

"You're right, I do." Jamie studied her long enough that she fought the urge to squirm. "Seen Topher lately?"

"I told you we were hanging out."

"Yeah. And you told me he followed you on a two hour road trip just to have a few minutes with you. Because he's hooked. Are you giving the guy a break or no?"

"Why are you so interested in my love life? Should I tell Mom to bump it up to texting you four phone numbers a day?"

Jamie shuddered. "Please don't. Although she's now started including links to social media, so I can look at pictures. The crop today wasn't awful."

"Where is she finding this many single girls in the right age range?" Vanessa held up a finger. "Hold that thought, that sounds like the food."

"They're quick."

Vanessa shrugged. Some nights they were. Others not so much. Tuesdays were, apparently, not their crazy day. She flipped on the light in the front room and unlocked the door with a smile. "Hey, Carrie. Thanks."

"Got a guest tonight?" The teenager snapped her gum and waggled her eyebrows.

"Just my brother." She reached for the bag. "Make sure you get your tip, I added it in the app."

The girl patted her pocket where, presumably, her phone was. "Already set. Have a nice night."

"You too." Vanessa relocked the door and gave it a push to be sure everything was latched before heading back. "Hungry?"

"You know it." Jamie closed the lid of the box he'd been peeking into. "Those are cool—kind of iridescent."

"Peacock Hill. Peacock feathers. It seemed like a good way to go. I have this design for the arrangement to sort of fan out like the tail." Vanessa shrugged and pushed papers out of the way before setting down the paper bag full of food. "I guess we'll see if I can pull it off or not."

"My money's on you. Or it would be, if I was still a person who bet on things. New leaf here though, promise." Jamie held up two fingers.

"I thought it was three fingers."

Jamie shrugged and reached for the bag of food. "Never was a very good scout. All that camping? Yuck."

"Says the man who lived homeless for how long again?"

"Yeah, well." Jamie shrugged out of his suit jacket and hung it over the back of a chair. "You can do a lot of things you never thought you'd do when it doesn't seem like there are any other options."

Vanessa slid a container of pot stickers to him and rummaged at the bottom of the bag for the paper-covered chopsticks and soy sauce. "I kissed him. Or he kissed me. Maybe it was mutual."

Jamie paused with a pot sticker halfway to his mouth. He set it back down. "So. Not a fake relationship after all."

She shook her head and dunked her own pot sticker before taking a bite.

"Serious?"

Was it? It could be. She wanted it to be. "I think maybe?"

"You've known him how long?"

"Close to two years. No. Closer to three, I guess." Had it been that long? It had. He was always showing up at weddings where she did the flowers. They'd both expanded into weddings about the same time—or so it seemed. "But we didn't do a lot of talking that first year. And after that, we didn't get along very well."

"Sure. Hate at first sight. It's a classic. You've seen Phantom of the Opera. You know that hate can turn to love."

Vanessa laughed as her brother sang the last words in what he probably thought was a spectral sounding voice. "Don't quit your day job. I don't think Broadway is going to be calling you anytime soon."

"Harsh."

"True."

"Yeah yeah. Still. Topher, huh?"

"What? I thought you liked him." Hadn't he been the one just last week urging her to go ahead and make it a real relationship?

"I do. And, bonus, maybe this gets Dad to unlock the rest of your trust."

"I'm not . . . I can't worry about that. I do okay. If this is what I have for the rest of my life, it's enough. It's more than a lot of people have." The money would be nice. She couldn't lie to herself about that. The charity could use a bigger infusion of cash than she managed with any regularity just from profits of the flower shop. She also wouldn't mind being a bit choosier about what weddings she took. Vanessa sighed. "I'm doing okay, Jamie. I really am."

"You can't expect me not to be upset that my bad decisions hurt you."

"Maybe not. But you need to try to let it go. For me."

He winced. "That's low."

"It isn't. I'm good. Money isn't everything, you know?" It had taken her long enough to come around to that. The first couple of years after Dad had made the change were embarrassing. She'd been so consumed by the desire to meet the terms of the trust that she'd flirted constantly. Not subtly. For a while she'd been on the verge of becoming someone she didn't recognize. Or like.

"Sure. But it makes things easier, you have to admit that."

Vanessa shrugged. "Some stuff, sure. Other stuff it makes harder. Right now, I'm trying to learn to be content like the Apostle Paul talks about. I have a lot more than so many people —I'm not going to wish I had even more."

Jamie pointed his chopsticks at her. "That's what makes you the best of all of us, you know that?"

Heat flooded her face and she shook her head. "I'm not better than anyone. Mom and Dad do a lot of good with their money. Sure, they spend it on themselves, too, but have you ever looked into how much they give away? It was eye opening."

"I only recently realized that because I ran across some of the accounts while I looking for something else at work. How'd you find out?"

"I asked."

Jamie laughed. "I guess that's one way. Topher doesn't mind?"

Vanessa frowned and tried to connect the thought processes. "Why would Topher mind that I asked Mom and Dad about their giving?"

"Not that. About the money in general. He knows you have money, right?"

"He's been to Mom and Dad's, so I'm guessing he pieced that together."

Jamie shook his head. "Not Mom and Dad. You. You, Vanessa Fisher, have money."

"But I don't. Not really. I manage a well-funded charity and I run a flower shop that makes a reasonable profit and is run out of a building I own. There's a potential for me to have more money. Certainly, I'll inherit quite a bit in another what, forty years? Unless Mom and Dad follow through on their threat to spend it all."

Jamie grinned. "They're still doing that whole 'Being of sound mind, I spent it all' wheeze? Nice."

"Dad thinks it's hilarious. Point being, what am I supposed to tell Topher?"

He drummed his fingers on the table top. "If it was me, I'd mention the trust fund. You'll still get the third tier, right? Dad didn't put any strings on it."

She'd completely forgotten about the third disbursement. That wasn't set up to hit until she was forty-five. That was fifteen years away. Might as well be a million. "Not yet. Who knows what'll happen when I miss the marriage deadline?"

"You think you'll miss it?"

"Topher . . . it hasn't even been a week yet and you think there's even a remote chance we'll be married by my birthday?"

"Engaged. Pretty sure you said you just have to be engaged.

And that's not unreasonable. You've known each other for a while. By the time your birthday rolls around you'll have, what, five months of dating under your belt? No one would bat an eye. Especially since you're turning thirty. It might raise eyebrows if you were nineteen, but come on, Nessa, think it through."

Put like that, maybe it was possible. In a highly theoretical situation. Was there any possibility Topher was thinking like that? It was still too soon. Much too soon. To get engaged, you had to be in love. To be in love? Well, she wasn't one hundred percent sure what made that happen, but there had to be something specific, didn't there? "We weren't friends."

"What?"

"For those three years. Topher and I weren't friends, remember? Phantom of the Opera?"

Jamie grinned. "Hatred to disguise the pain of unrequited love."

"You've lost your mind." Vanessa shook her head. There was no way Topher was in love with her.

It was a ridiculous thought.

Why did she want it to be possible?

20

Topher glanced over at Vanessa and smiled before turning his attention to the lock on the empty storefront. He was already close to admitting he needed to give up the idea of expanding, but his real estate agent friend had convinced him to give this location a look. "I really appreciate you coming to see this with me. I know it's not the most exciting excursion."

"You're kidding, right? I love looking at empty buildings. House, stores, whatever—it's fun to see what could be, and what other people have done with something. Before I bought my shop, I must have looked at close to everything that was available in Richmond. Much to the dismay of my agent."

He chuckled. "I'll admit my friend is getting a little frustrated. I think she was hoping to have a big commission before Christmas. It doesn't seem likely at this point."

"Ah, but she can drop a key off for you and stay home, or work with another client. So that's a win for her."

"Win for me, too." He opened the door and gestured for Vanessa to go in. Was there anyone who wanted a constant conversation about the inflated positives of a property? Topher reached over and grabbed Vanessa's hand.

She started, then relaxed and curved her fingers around his, glancing over with a smile. "This one's smaller."

"Out front, yes." Topher gave a little tug toward the counter and the door behind it which should, if the listing he'd been sent was accurate, reveal a much more suitable kitchen. "Let's see what's hiding in the back."

"Can I ask you something?"

"Sure. Do I need to be worried?" It wasn't generally a good thing when a woman started a conversation that way.

"No." She paused. "Well, maybe. A little. It's not serious."

"Uh-huh. Just ask."

"When we first met, did you hate me?"

"No." He squeezed her hand, let go, and crossed the large kitchen space to look more closely at the ovens. They were almost adequate. He'd have to replace them eventually, but if he bought this space he could open without doing a complete kitchen renovation right off. Of course, that meant down the line he'd have to close to do one, and that was never as good for business as starting out right. It was the continual question in business—spend now, or spend later?

"Dislike?"

He turned at the irritation in her voice and fought a sigh. "When we first met, I thought you were attractive. Then you got irritated with me and I thought it was too bad that was your personality. Then I got to know you better and realized that irritating persona was just that, something you put on whenever you dealt with me, and not who you really were. Now that I've seen the real you, I love who you really are."

Vanessa blinked and her mouth gaped.

"You asked." He turned and looked at the walk-in refrigerator. He could practically feel Vanessa's eyes burning into his back, like laser beams. But she'd asked! He wasn't going to lie. Maybe he should have.

"You think I'm irritating."

He turned, head shaking. "Thought. As in 'no longer my current opinion'. Although I do find it fascinating that that's what you glommed on to when I also said I love you."

"No." She took a step back. "You said you loved the real me."

He nodded. How was that different? If anything, wasn't it better?

"As opposed to the irritating person I was when we first met."

"Tell me honestly you didn't also find me annoying." Topher crossed his arms. Would she lie? Because if she said anything other than he was right, he'd know it for the untruth that it was. Sean had come to him plenty of times with yet another complaint by Vanessa.

"Fine. Yes. I did." She scooped her hands through her hair.

Topher stepped in close and put his hands on her shoulders. "What's going on?"

"My brother. He came by on Tuesday and said some things and . . ." Vanessa blew out a breath. "You know my parents are rich."

He gave a slow nod. Where was this going? "I'm not sure what that has to do with anything."

"Just wait." Vanessa took a deep breath. "So. There's a trust fund. Family tradition says the first tier is always used to set up a business and then start a charity. So that's what I did. I bought the building for my shop, and the rest is set up to help women get their feet under them. We work a lot with pregnancy resource centers and non-traditional schools. Doesn't matter. The point is, I don't consider that money mine. It isn't. It's God's."

"Okay." Where was she going with this? "That's admirable."

"There's more." Vanessa took a step back and turned away. "There's another disbursement when I'm thirty. So, February. But when Jamie took off and started squandering his, Dad made some changes. I only get the money if I'm engaged."

His ears started buzzing. What was she saying? "I see."

"I don't think you do." Vanessa turned and stepped closer, twisting her fingers together. "I don't care about the money. I wasn't going to say anything to you about it, even, but Jamie seemed to think you needed to know—that it would be worse, somehow, if you found out after the fact. I told him there was no way we'd be engaged by my birthday—no matter what I feel for you or you think you feel for me, we haven't been dating that long and it all started as a way to get Mom off my back with the ball, so I keep expecting you to decide that's the end of it anyway, but I also didn't want to lie. And leaving it out . . . that would be a lie, right?"

Bits and pieces of what she said pushed their way through the noise in his head, but he couldn't quite grab onto any one of the thoughts to make a response.

"Topher?" Vanessa angled her head to meet his gaze. "Say something. Please?"

"We—we should go. I don't think this space is going to work."

Vanessa drew in a shaky breath and nodded. "Right. Okay. Sure."

Topher switched off the kitchen lights, his thoughts reeling. He paused by the main door and scraped together enough coherency to speak. "One thing. What I feel for you isn't something I imagined."

"I HAVE TO ADMIT, I thought you'd be on a date with Vanessa

tonight." Sean grabbed a handful of chips out of the bag on Topher's coffee table and popped them into his mouth one by one.

"Yeah. That was my thinking, too." Brian frowned and reached for the chips. "Why is it that I broke a first date to come eat stale chips on your sofa?"

Topher dropped a little velvet box on the table next to the bag and sat on the couch between his friends. "That's why."

Sean whistled and reached for the box. "When did you get this?"

"Saw it Sunday when you and I went to look. I went back on Tuesday to get it." He shook his head. Tuesday. The same day Vanessa's brother was explaining to her that she needed to be honest about who she was.

"Why aren't you out on a date and giving her this?" Brian held out his hand for the box. His eyebrows lifted when Sean handed it over. "This is some ring."

Topher took the ring back and stared at it for a moment before snapping the lid shut. Then he filled his friend in on the conversation he and Vanessa had had last night. "Now what?"

"Secret rich girl." Brian laughed and grabbed more chips. "That's cool."

Sean shifted to face Topher. "Does it change anything?"

"Of course it does. What if she decided she needed that money after all, so she looked around for the first available sucker and oh, hey, how about Topher?" Topher flopped back on the couch and stared at the ceiling. The what-ifs had kept him up half the night. The little sleep he'd managed had been restless and broken. "And I fell for it."

"If she was doing that, why did she tell you? She had to know you'd wonder. Unless she's stupid, and that doesn't seem like someone you'd go for." Brian took another chip and frowned at the coffee table. "Don't you at least have salsa? Or queso? Something to make these not taste like soggy dust?"

"Check the fridge." Topher waved toward the kitchen. Everything tasted like cardboard today. Salsa wasn't going to help.

"You have to admit Brian has a point." Sean took another handful of chips.

"I told her I loved her. Maybe she realized it was working and had a moment of conscience." Topher scrubbed a hand over his face. "I don't know. I don't even know how to figure it out."

Brian came back with a jar of salsa and a bowl. "I'll be the first to admit that, of the three of us, I know the least about women. But I do know relationships. So I have to ask, why don't you just talk to her about it?"

"Oh, sure. Be reasonable and mature." Topher sighed and dunked a chip in the salsa. "I need to do that. I will. I thought it might be a good plan to know what I thought about it beforehand though."

"That's not a terrible thought. I took a few days to think through all the issues with Larissa before I committed to pursuing her. There's always going to be baggage though. Part of loving someone is being willing to work through the ups and downs. Together."

Brian nodded. "That's wise. Listen to the wedding guy."

Sean grinned. "Have you prayed about it?"

"Some. Maybe not enough. I don't know how much is me and how much is the Holy Spirit."

"Are you hearing different things?" Sean poked the tip of a chip into the salsa and sniffed it before crunching down.

"Not really. I always circle back to asking myself why money would change anything. It shouldn't. I'm doing well—well enough that I'm considering opening a second location. And she does well enough now without the money."

"Would it change her?" Brian leaned forward. "I don't know

her, so I can't tell you what I think, but is she the kind of person who becomes someone else when there's money involved?"

Was she? Vanessa was different at her parents' house. Some of that—most of it, even—was because of her relationship with them. They were still struggling to find their way to that elusive parent-to-adult-child understanding. His parents had swung one way and were, for all practical purposes, uninvolved in his life unless he made the effort. Which he didn't do as often as he ought. He knew they loved him. He loved them. But there wasn't any sort of day-to-day, or even week-to-week communication. Vanessa's parents, or her mom, at least, seemed to have gone the other direction, wanting to be even more involved than if Vanessa still lived at home. Was that a function of gender? Her brother's rebellion?

Probably some combination of them all.

Even with all that in the mix, Topher couldn't say Vanessa was someone who appeared to care about money. Wouldn't she have asked more about Topher's business details if she was? He'd given her opportunities by taking her along to look at additional spaces. She'd never once questioned.

"No. I don't think she is."

"Then I don't see why it matters. If you love her without the money, why should that change just because she's suddenly rich?" Brian shook more salsa into the bowl.

"He has a point." Sean reached for the bag of chips. "And since we're back to that—you love her? That seems sudden."

Topher laughed. Leave it to Sean to just blurt things out. "Maybe. I don't know. It doesn't feel that way to me."

"Uh-huh. Just over a month ago you were complaining about her to me, remember that? Azure and Matt's Labor Day wedding at Peacock Hill?"

"She can be annoying. I can love her and still recognize that she's sometimes seriously annoying. Can't I?"

Brian snickered. "If you can't, then I've never been in love."

"All right, fine. My point still holds though. A little over a month."

"And three years of working together off and on before that. It's not like I met her for the first time six weeks ago. Maybe we weren't friends who hung out all the time, but I knew her. Don't you think at some point you just know? It's not like we're eighteen and still trying to figure out life. I'll be thirty two next year, she'll be thirty. We're not kids. Bottom line? She loves Jesus, which is my number one criterion for a potential mate. We're good friends now, whatever we were before, and when I try to imagine my life without her in it? I don't want to go there." That was enough, wasn't it? It was certainly a solid foundation on which to build a life together.

"Then you need to talk to her. And let me be the first to say congratulations." Sean shook his head. "How is it that I bought a ring before you but you're going to end up engaged first?"

"Don't bet on that. When I told her that I loved her, she accused me of imagining things."

21

Vanessa parked the shop van in front of the main entrance to Peacock Hill. The sun was already sinking below the mountains, sending spears of orange and pink across the sky. But it couldn't have been helped. Even though they were just over two weeks out from the Founder's Ball, she couldn't close the shop in the middle of the week. And so she'd ended up driving out as soon as she'd locked the door.

She should have waited until the weekend.

Except Topher would have offered to tag along. She wasn't ready to see Topher yet.

Claire skipped down the steps, grinning. "Hey, you made it."

Vanessa hopped out and opened the back doors. "Just about on time, at that. I appreciate you letting me bring these down now. My back room just isn't big enough to store everything for the next two weeks."

"It's all good. I'm looking forward to seeing them in place."

Vanessa reached in for one of the boxes holding the giant, iridescent, floor-standing vases she'd ordered for the ball. "We can open one up when we get them in, if you want. Where did you want me to put the boxes?"

Clare hefted a box and started up the steps. "I'll show you. They're heavier than I thought."

They always were. Vanessa never quite understood how people didn't piece together the idea that something designed to hold a large flower arrangement had to have some heft of its own to avoid being broken or tipped over. She had at least learned enough to stop saying that out loud.

She followed Claire into the mansion, turning left almost immediately. The room featured floor to ceiling windows facing the front lawn. Currently, a loveseat and two chairs were arranged in a small conversational grouping off to one side. "You don't use this room?"

"We can't agree on what it should be." Claire set the box down against the far wall and shrugged. "I think we ought to set up smaller tables with chairs and make it an informal eating area that allows privacy. Right now, we have the big table in the dining room and everyone has to gather around it. But if we get smaller groups, like this writer retreat, or even individuals who want to do a solo retreat, they aren't always going to want to eat at a communal table, right?"

Vanessa nodded. She could kind of see that. "Sure. There's the breakfast room though?"

Claire laughed. "Which is what Deidre says. She keeps talking about moving the business center up here. Then there'd be no reason for guests to go into the basement. It's not a terrible idea—and I like the idea of making that space completely off limits—but is that really the first room you want to walk into? Plus, if we did that, there's no chance of using this space for smaller indoor weddings."

"Were you planning on doing that?" Vanessa headed back toward the front door. There were quite a few more boxes to bring in.

"Not specifically. So far all the brides have opted for outside or they've wanted the foyer so they can enter by coming down the staircase."

"You have to admit the stairs are amazing." Vanessa could picture herself in a fancy dress gliding down those stairs, light shining through the stained glass behind her. "It's definitely an entrance with that hard-to-define wow factor."

"Sure, if you're into that kind of thing."

"Who isn't? Come on, Claire, it's like something out of a fairy tale."

Claire shrugged and grabbed another box. "I guess. I just think it'd be nice to have another option to offer. Moving café seating is a lot easier than packing up computers and office tables."

"I guess you don't need another space to hang out." Vanessa set the box down with a glance at the small conversational grouping. "You've got the room behind here with sofas and a TV, right?"

"Yeah." Claire put her box down and started back toward the front door. "So for now we have this. Which is fine. Right now, no one needs the space. I'd just love to know there was a solid plan for it before I left."

Vanessa frowned and hurried to catch up with Claire on the steps. "You're still thinking of going? Even with the ball?"

"Deidre doesn't need me. With the baby, it's not like she's going to be taking on any big renovations off site. It makes a lot of sense for her to transition into the event management role here. Jeremiah can still do any of the handyman stuff that Dee doesn't have time to handle. Duncan and Anna are here for whatever falls through the cracks. Even with their landscaping business starting to take off. And if something major happened, Matt and Azure are here in town too. Nobody needs me."

"I think you're wrong, but I understand the feeling." Vanessa hefted the next box. "You should talk to your sister and explain."

Claire shook her head. "Speaking of the ball, when are you going to need to set up? I've got people starting on Thursday, if you can believe it."

"I can do it Saturday morning and afternoon. It's better if I'm close to the end, anyway. That way no one decides they need to move an arrangement—that never ends well." Vanessa couldn't stop the smile as she remembered the various arguments she and Topher had had over the years because of exactly that. What did it say about her—about them—that even those encounters left her warm inside?

"What's funny?"

Vanessa shook her head. There was no possible way to explain it and sound sane.

"I kind of expected Topher would come down with you." Claire waggled her eyebrows. "He busy tonight?"

There were only two more boxes. Vanessa sighed and sat on the edge of the van's cargo area. "I didn't ask him. I'm kind of avoiding him right now. He wants to talk—and he's right, we need to—but I'm not sure I want to."

"Because?" Claire perched next to her.

"Because I don't know what's going to happen? The whole 'we need to talk' thing is scary." Maybe at twenty nine that was ridiculous, but if there was a more ominous phrase in the English language, Vanessa didn't know what it was.

"You don't have any idea what he wants to talk about? It just came out of the blue?"

"Not quite. I . . ." This was the problem with having friends. Once all these people were involved, they had to all get the information. Vanessa sighed. "My parents are pretty wealthy."

"Okay."

"Like I have a trust fund wealthy." She fought the urge to cringe as she waited for Claire's response.

"So Topher just found out he's dating a billionaire? It's like a

romance novel." Claire started to laugh and made fake head-
lines with her hands as she continued to talk. "'The Secret
Billionaire's Baker Boyfriend' or, wait, I know, 'Dating the Secret
Billionaire.' Or maybe simpler, 'A Baker for the Billionaire.'"

"Har, har, har. I'm not a billionaire." Yet. Even with her trust
fund fully kicked in she wouldn't be. Until her father died. Then,
when all was said and done, if she were to include the value of
her stock in her dad's company, it'd be close. Provided there
wasn't a business crash between now and whenever she inher-
ited. Why was she even thinking about this?

"Millionaire, then. Just as good." Claire chuckled. "Why is
this a problem? He can't think you're after him for his money."

"I suspect he thinks I'm after him because of it. There's a
hangup with the trust and I only get the next bit if I'm engaged
by my thirtieth."

Claire gaped. "No way. That's medieval."

"That's my dad. He thinks he's looking out for me and
keeping me from making the same mistakes my brother made
when he turned thirty. The thing is, I'd basically written the
money off. I realized that any guy I could get to propose just to
make Dad's arbitrary deadline wasn't someone worth pursuing.
So I quit looking."

"And that made you all the more attractive. I know how guys
are. Disinterest is the quickest way to make a guy think he's in
love. Unless you're Danny. Then it backfires."

"You tried to reverse psychology Danny into dating you?"

"Seemed like a good idea at the time." Claire shook her
head. "But we aren't talking about me. You don't know Topher's
going to throw you over just because you have money."

No. She didn't know that. That was part of the problem. "He
said he loves me."

"Before or after he found out about the money."

"Before."

"So why would that change?"

"Why wouldn't it? How does he even know he loves me? We haven't been together long enough to be in love. That has to take at least, what, six months?"

Claire laughed. "Says who?"

"Everyone. Seriously, if I told you about some random friend of mine who was head over heels in love with someone after, generously, six weeks of dating, you'd think they were crazy."

"Not necessarily. If you were in high school, sure, maybe even college. But you're both adults. You have careers and a life. One could extrapolate that you know what you want out of life and a mate. I'm not saying decide to love the first person who asks you out who ticks those boxes, but when you find someone who does and who you get along with? I don't think you should walk away because you're scared." Claire stood and dragged the second to last box closer. "At least be sure before you throw it away. He said he loves you. That should count for something."

Vanessa watched Claire carry the box up the stairs and mulled her words. There were valid points in there. Not that Vanessa's concerns were unfounded or wrong, but the reality was, she didn't know what Topher wanted to say.

And she missed him.

She shouldn't—couldn't—discount that.

He'd come to mean a lot in a very short space of time.

Vanessa sighed and stood, grabbing the last box. She wasn't sure if she loved him.

But she'd like to.

There was a stampede of wild horses running circles in her stomach. Vanessa fought the urge to pace as she second-guessed the low-heeled boots she'd pulled on when she'd changed into dark jeans and a sweater after closing the shop. After talking to Claire on Wednesday night, she hadn't been able to continue avoiding Topher. They were adults. It was time to act like it.

Apparently he'd come to the same conclusion, because he texted her just as she was working up the nerve to reach out to him. So he was picking her up and they were going to a local pumpkin patch. She smiled. Who thought of doing that as adults? Especially adults with no kids. She hadn't been to something like that since college—and even then they'd gone as a joke, mostly.

There was a knock—finally! Vanessa forced herself to walk at a normal pace to the door.

Topher held out a single pink rose. "Hi."

Her heart melted. "Hi, yourself. You look good."

"Thanks. So do you." He cleared his throat. "This is awkward. I didn't want it to be awkward. I'm sorry. I could have handled it—everything—better. Should have. I don't want to lose you. When I told you I loved you, I meant it. I know it got lost in the middle of stuff, but that doesn't make it less real."

"Why don't you come in? I have a bud vase for that rose." She reached for the blossom that he still clenched in his fist. "Before it gets too mangled."

"Right. Ha." He followed her to the kitchen.

Vanessa nearly bumped into him when she turned from filling a tall, skinny crystal vase with water. She snipped the bottom of the rose's stem and dropped it into the water. "You're not the only one who didn't handle it well. I've spent most of my adult life trying to avoid being lumped into the trust fund baby category—at least when I wasn't making a fool of myself trying to flirt with anyone I could to try and meet the terms of Dad's addendum. Then, when I finally realized no amount of money was worth that, I stopped even wanting to think about it, let alone talk to people about it. I don't want to lose you because of money."

"Not going to happen." Topher closed the distance between them and touched his lips to hers. "And, for the record, I don't feel pressured to propose before your birthday because of the money, either."

Vanessa ignored the tinge of hysteria that coated the edges of her laugh. "Good. I'd hate for you to feel like you had to do something—anything—when it comes to us. We can wait and see what God has for us."

He nodded. "I've been praying for you—for us—for a while now."

He had? She did, when she thought about it. Unfortunately, that summed up her prayer life in general. She tended to act and, when all else failed, pray. It was something she was working on. "I need to do better at that."

Topher took her hand. "We can work on it together. You ready to go?"

"Yeah. Okay. Pumpkin patch, huh? What gave you that idea?" Vanessa snagged her purse from the table by the door.

"I go every year. Usually with Sean or a group of guys from the bakery. It's a good activity for all ages. In the evening, like this, there won't be as many families with younger kids, but the teens will be out. Some are there with parents, others with youth groups or just a collection of friends." Topher pulled open the passenger door of his car for Vanessa. "It's fun. The corn maze at night is harder, and sometimes there are workers who pop out of the corn to scare you."

"Um. Yay?"

Topher laughed and closed the door.

She waited until he was backing out of the parking space before she spoke again. "I don't really love scary."

"Seriously? It's a corn maze with ridiculous costumes. It's not scary. Startling, maybe." He glanced over at her, a slight frown on his face. "But if you're worried, we can do the maze first. They don't do any of the extras until it's full dark."

Maybe it was ridiculous, but Halloween was her least favorite holiday. Dressing up as a kid and begging for candy had been fun, but as she'd aged, everything seemed to turn darker, focusing on the scary. She'd tried one horror movie with friends in high school and after three weeks of nightmares finally concluded there was no point in even pretending to be cool when it came to the end of October. "You don't mind?"

"Nah. If you don't want to do anything scary, we don't have to. We'll do the maze, find some of the slides, and then take a hay ride."

"That sounds nice. Thanks." She turned and looked out the window as he wound his way out of the city. "Is there more to say about the trust fund?"

"Not if you don't want to talk about it."

It wasn't that she didn't want to. She just didn't know what to say. "It's not that."

"Then we'll leave it alone for now. I love you, Vanessa."

She smiled and reached over to touch his knee. She wanted to say the words to him, but they got lodged in her chest.

What was wrong with her?

22

Topher poured batter into cake pans and pushed them aside. If only it was as easy to get his thoughts to stop circling around. Vanessa. What was he going to do about her? It's not like he expected her to automatically respond when he told her loved her, but some kind of acknowledgment that she cared for him beyond what she felt for a friend would be nice. But no. He got a smile and a pat on the knee.

What did that mean?

Shaking his head, he carried the pans to the oven and loaded them in. Focus on the baking. He could control that. And maybe, just maybe, somewhere in the whirling thoughts, God would break through and help him understand what he was supposed to do. Because he could really use the guidance.

"Hey, boss?"

Topher set a timer and turned to see the new girl—Marcy?—poking her head in from the front of the bakery. "Yeah?"

"There's a guy here who says he's your friend?"

"Okay. I'll be right out." He washed his hands and tried to figure out who would visit him at the bakery. It wasn't unheard of, but most of his friends worked regular hours, making daytime shop visits unlikely. After a glance at his apron to ensure it wasn't too dirty, he pushed through the swinging door into the retail space.

"Hey, man." Brian lifted a hand holding a cookie. "These are great. I don't know that I realized you made cookies, too."

"It's a bakery." Topher skirted the end of the counter with a nod to Marcy. "What did you think we made?"

"Cakes. French pastries with weird names. Obscure stuff."

He laughed. "We make those, too. You pay for that?"

Brian rolled his eyes. "Of course. And coffee, but she just gave me a cup."

Topher pointed to the self-service coffee area wedged in the corner of the small eating area. "Other than our amazing cookies, what brings you out this way?"

"I don't know. I needed to get out of the office for a bit—ended up here. You were busy with Vanessa all weekend."

It wasn't a question, but Topher nodded anyway. "Why don't you bring that in the back? I need to be where I can hear some timers."

"It's not too crowded?"

"Not this time of day. We're down to the two out front and me in the back right now. Come on." Topher considered a moment before striding to the register and grabbing himself a coffee cup. He could use a jolt of caffeine. He filled the cup, splashed in a little creamer from the jug sitting nearby, and headed toward the back, holding the door for Brian.

"Wow. It's all shiny."

Topher laughed. "We do try for cleanliness here in the food service industry."

"Ha ha. I guess I imagined there would be something that wasn't stainless steel back here."

Topher surveyed the space, trying to imagine what it looked like to someone who didn't need a commercial kitchen and failed. It was what he needed—he'd spent enough time and money getting it designed just so when he first opened the bakery—that it ought to be. The first year had been a month-by-month nail biter, trying to figure out if he was going to sell enough to meet all the payments he had to make. The second year hadn't been much better, though there had been enough constant business that it hadn't produced as much anxiety. Every year since had been better than the last, which was why he was considering expanding. He finished his coffee and tossed the cup in the trash before heading to the sink to wash his hands again.

"It smells good in here."

"That's the cake that's in the oven. Four graduated octagonal tiers for a Friday night wedding. Simple white fondant with purple fondant violets and a satin ribbon to be provided on site at setup."

"That's all in your head?"

Topher nodded. "It's what I'm working on right now, so sure. That's not amazing. What's really going on?"

Brian sighed and sipped his coffee. "Dave wants to get together and talk."

"Hmm. Will you?"

"I don't know what to do. What would you do?"

"That's hard to answer."

"Can you try? I don't want to throw away everything we had. But I also don't want to be a sucker."

"It probably wouldn't hurt to talk to him face-to-face. If you can keep things civil. You've talked on the phone some already and managed."

Brian nodded. "Him, too."

"You can only control what you do, man. But if you're going

to scream and yell, there's no point. Can you listen to what he has to say?"

"I guess. Look at you, all reasonable. Why did you say it was hard to answer?"

"It goes back to how much I want you to find Jesus. So while I do think it's worthwhile to listen to Dave and see if you can salvage your friendship, at least, I also recognize that solidifying your relationship with him is going to close the door on Jesus, at least for now. Because whatever you do, I'm not going to stop being your friend. And I'm not going to stop praying for you." Topher brushed at non-existent crumbs on the counter. He wanted something to do with his hands. Something else to focus on.

"Okay. I . . . am trying to remember that you've never pulled your punches with me."

Topher looked up and bit his lip when he saw the hurt etched in his friend's face. "I'm sorry. I know that's not exactly what you wanted me to say."

"No, it isn't. But you know what? It's still the most honest answer I've gotten. Did you fix things with your girl, Vanessa, right?"

"I think so."

"You think so. Seems to me this is a yes or no situation. What happened?" Brian tossed his cup toward the trash and it bounced off the rim. He shook his head and crossed to the trash to pick up the cup and drop it in.

"We talked. The money thing isn't an issue. Let me ask you a question."

"Okay."

"If someone tells you they love you, what do you do?"

Brian lifted his eyebrows. "Give me some context. Is this pillow talk or something else?"

"Dude. You know me. It's not pillow talk."

"Right, right. Sorry. I forgot I was talking to Mr. Purity."

Topher sighed. "Never mind."

"No, hey, don't be mad. I'm sorry—that was a low blow. Um, okay, so it's not inappropriate timing, like a first date, right?"

"Right."

"Then I guess I say I love you back. Unless I don't feel that way, in which case I try to let the guy down easy. Maybe smile or say something non-committal like 'thank you'."

"Where does a smile and a pat on the knee fall?"

Brian winced.

Topher nodded. "That's what I figured. So what do I do?"

"You're asking the wrong guy, though it seems to me you ought to do what you're probably already doing."

"What's that?"

"Pray about it. I'm not one for prayer myself—but it seems to work for you. I know your life has made me reconsider my stance a number of times."

That was something, at least. "All right, I'll just keep praying. It's good advice."

Brian laughed. "Don't tell anyone you got it from me. My rep will get ruined."

"Mum's the word. You'll keep me posted on the Dave situation?"

"You know it." Brian checked his phone and blew out a breath. "I should run. A break is one thing, disappearing for the afternoon is another."

"Grab another cookie on your way out. Tell them I said it was okay."

"Yeah? Thanks. Later."

Topher watched his friend leave and rubbed the back of his neck. Prayer was the right answer. He knew that. Sometimes it would just be nice if there was an answer that was easier. But that would probably defeat the purpose.

"Appreciate you making the drive out." Vanessa's father reached out to shake Topher's hand. His grip was firm—firmer than Topher remembered it being.

"Not a problem. Is there somewhere you wanted me to put the desserts? Some of them will do better in a refrigerator until it's time to serve." Vanessa's mother had called on Tuesday afternoon to see if it was possible for him to provide a few fancy desserts for a party they were hosting on Friday night. Since he had a wedding already on Friday, he couldn't do day-of delivery —or stay for the party as she'd invited him to do—but he'd seen no reason he couldn't make the food and bring it Thursday if that worked for them. It did.

"Oh, just set it in the kitchen. Estelle will take care of getting it all stored. There's a second, larger fridge, in the pantry. With all the entertaining we do, it makes more sense. When you're set, have Estelle show you to my study, would you?"

That didn't sound ominous. Not at all. He forced a smile. "Sounds good."

James gave a nod and disappeared down the hall.

Okay then. Topher headed back to his car and grabbed the first of two insulated boxes from his trunk. He made his way to the kitchen, taking only one wrong turn along the way. Was he supposed to have remembered it perfectly from the one time he'd been here? He slid the box on the counter and retraced his steps to the car.

When he returned to the kitchen, Estelle was busy unpacking the first box. She looked up with a grin. "These tortes look good enough to eat."

He laughed and slid the second box on the counter. "That's the idea. Can I help?"

"Oh, no. I have a system. Any time a man tries to help me, things get messed up."

Topher held up his hands and took a step back. "I promise not to touch. The second box doesn't need refrigeration. They should be fine at room temperature until tomorrow night."

"Is it better if they're cool?"

"It won't hurt them."

She gave a brisk nod. "Then I'll put them in the fridge with the rest, that way nothing gets forgotten."

"Okay." He tucked his hands in his pockets and glanced over his shoulder toward the hall. "I'm supposed to find Mr. Fisher in his study?"

"I'll take you." Estelle wiped her hands on a towel and patted his arm as she passed him. "You just follow me."

It didn't take long—nor was it a particularly difficult room to find. Estelle rapped briskly on the door before pushing it open a crack. "Topher's here."

"Come in, come in. Thanks, Estelle." James stood behind his desk, hands clasped behind his back. "Pull that door closed behind you, son, and have a seat."

Topher did as instructed, settling in one of the leather club chairs facing the massive desk.

James sat and steepled his fingers. "Really do appreciate you handling the desserts for us. I know it was short notice."

"It's not a big deal. We had the time." And since Vanessa's mother hadn't made any specific requests beyond the number of people, he'd chosen simpler things that just looked fancy. "I'm always glad when I can help people I know."

"Hmm. People you know."

Topher nodded.

"How are things going with my daughter?"

He raised his eyebrows. That had come out of left field.

Although, maybe if he'd been thinking it would have occurred to him that the man would ask. "Fine, I guess."

James pressed his lips together. "That's not exactly what I was hoping to hear. My son said she explained about her trust."

"She did."

"And?"

Topher fought the urge to shift in his seat. "And I think it's nice that she has a cushion for her future."

"You think she'll meet the stipulations, then?"

This time he did fidget. "I love your daughter, sir. I'm not sure she feels the same way about me, but I hope, given time, she might decide she does."

"And then?"

"Then I hope she'll agree to marry me."

James grunted. "Do I have any say in the matter?"

"Well, to be honest, I don't think so, sir. Neither of us are kids. It would be nice, certainly, to have your blessing, but if you were to say you didn't approve, I'd still ask her. And I think, knowing what I do about Vanessa, she'd still say yes. When we get to that point."

Now he laughed, a loud barking sound. "You'd have to be stubborn to have any chance of a future with her. Not pandering to me will win you points there, as well. If I don't give my blessing, I could decide to stop the trust."

"That would be your choice. It wouldn't impact mine." Topher leaned forward and held James' gaze. "I fell in love with your daughter before I knew about any money. If that money disappears, that doesn't change anything. If she ends up a trillionaire, that isn't going to change things either. The only thing now that would make me walk away from Vanessa is if she asked me to. And I'd try to change her mind about that."

James nodded slowly. "I believe you mean that."

"I do."

"Very well. This shouldn't be a problem then." He pulled open a drawer and withdrew a folder. He flipped open the front flap, scanned the first page, then slid it across the desk to Topher.

Frowning, Topher pulled the document forward. A prenuptial agreement? He skimmed the words, working his way through the legalese. Why they insisted on so many wherefores and theretos he would never understand. He hated the idea of it. Marriage was meant to be a melding of two into one—in all areas. At the same time, he couldn't fault James for wanting to look after his daughter. That was, after all, his job. Though she might disagree. "Do you have a pen?"

"Just like that?" James plucked the pen from his shirt pocket and offered across the desk.

"I love Vanessa. I don't care particularly about her money. I suspect, if you were to ask her, you might find she doesn't care about it all that much either." Topher scrawled his name across the bottom of the last page and added the date. "Does that constitute your blessing?"

"It does."

"Well. That's something." Topher handed back the pen and stood. "I should get going. I hope you enjoy the desserts tomorrow night. I left the invoice on the kitchen counter."

"You're angry. That speaks well of you. I think you'll understand someday, when you have a daughter of your own."

Topher shook his head. "I hope not. If I'm blessed to have a daughter of my own, I hope and pray that I'll trust her to live out the precepts her mother and I instill in her during her childhood. To trust that she has a strong enough relationship with Jesus that her decisions are based on the leading of the Holy Spirit and not the manipulation of a man who is unworthy of her. Have a good evening."

James started to speak, but Topher had already thrown open

the study door and was striding toward the front entrance. There was a small corner of his mind that understood what James was trying to do—the love and concern that motivated it. The rest of him bristled. Not on his own behalf—let Vanessa keep the money. What did he care? No, he was angry for her. Vanessa was an amazing woman—personally and profession-ally. How devastated must she be to realize her father couldn't—wouldn't—see it?

23

Vanessa admired the simply decorated octagonal layers as Topher assembled the wedding cake in the small neighborhood clubhouse. "I think this might be my favorite cake of yours."

He glanced up and smiled. "Thanks. It was an easy one, comparatively speaking. Sometimes the simple ones stand out for just that reason."

"The flowers are straightforward as well, which is nice. I'm basically spending the whole of next week on the arrangements for the Founder's Ball, and not having two crazy weeks in a row was a real bonus." At some point she needed to find a dress. She'd managed to avoid caving to her mother's suggestions, but the reality was, nothing currently in her closet was going to do. Which meant shopping.

"You're frowning. Is there a problem?"

"Not really. Thinking about the ball made me remember I don't have a dress yet." Vanessa shrugged. "I'll get it handled this week one way or another."

"Is online an option?"

She laughed. "Only if I want to hear about it from my

mother for the next decade. That said, I may go that route for ease and worry about consequences later."

"Why would she care? Or even know?"

"She'd ask. I'm not going to lie—and then she'd go on and on about how she tried to help me when there was plenty of time still." Vanessa shrugged. "It's just the way my mom is. I remind myself she means well and acts this way because she loves me."

"Both your parents do." Topher settled the ceramic bride and groom on top of the cake and stepped back.

"They do. Sometimes I think too much. Or, that's not the right way to put it. Maybe their love hasn't adjusted to the idea that I'm a grown woman." Vanessa turned and looked across the small venue, her gaze shifting between the various arrangements she'd placed. "Doesn't matter. As nice as it would be for them to love me the way that I want them to, they're not going to change. So I just work to remind myself that they're doing the best they can and accept them for who they are."

Topher rounded the dessert table and slipped his arm around her shoulders. "Do I love you the way you want me to?"

She turned into him and wrapped her arms around his waist, tipping her head back."The fact that you love me at all is incredible."

He studied her for a moment before kissing her nose and stepping back. "Not from where I'm standing."

"Topher?"

"Yeah?"

"I care about you. You know that, right?"

"Sure." He rounded the table and flipped open a cooler. "I should get the rest of the desserts set out. Are you staying for this one?"

Sure? That was not the answer she'd been expecting. What was she supposed to do with that? Her experience with her parents suggested that "sure" meant anything but. She bit the inside of her cheek. "No. I'm set. They want to keep everything, so I don't have any cleanup."

"I have to stay and serve the cake. Busy tomorrow?"

"Yeah, I have to head out to my parents' house. They're having a family meeting—I'm sure it's to do with Jamie taking over Dad's company officially or something like that, but I still have to go. Church on Sunday?"

"Of course. Want me to pick you up?" Topher glanced up from arranging rows of glistening pastries.

"I'd like that."

Topher nodded. "Then I'll see you Sunday morning."

Vanessa twisted her fingers together. Something was off, but she didn't know how to fix it. Maybe it was because he was busy. Or having a bad day. Something not her fault. But that didn't seem super likely. He loved her. He was clearly waiting for her to tell him she felt the same way. But how was she supposed to know if what she felt was really love?

Stifling a sigh, she sent him a tiny wave and headed out to her car. It was early enough that she could hit up a dress shop on her way home. Might as well get the torture out of the way when she was already unhappy.

"I'm so glad you could come." Vanessa's mother pulled her into a tight hug, then leaned back. "Love looks good on you."

Vanessa managed a weak smile. "Thanks, Mom. I brought a picture of my dress for next week, would you like to see it?"

"Of course. After the meeting. Your father's impatient." Her mother rolled her eyes and gestured in the direction of the den.

Usually family meetings took place around the kitchen table. For all that her parents were formal, they had always worked to keep things comfortable. Was the den more intimidating? Or less? "Jamie's here?"

"He stayed last night."

Right. Their party. Mom had been annoyed, verging on angry, that Vanessa hadn't been able to attend, but there had been no way to handle the wedding and still make it out with any reasonable attendance at their shindig. "How was the get-together?"

"It was fine. Your brother made some good connections with friends of your father. None of the single women caught his eye, or, if they did, he didn't let on. Maybe he got a phone number or two. You should ask him about that."

"Me? Why me?"

"Because he told me I was nagging." Her mother sniffed. "As if wanting him to be settled and stable was somehow a bad thing."

"He's not going to run away again, Mom. He doesn't need a wife to ensure that." A wife wouldn't have stopped the first disappearance. Her brother would have dragged the woman along. Given the kinds of women he had been dating before he'd left, they might have been the instigator of the decision to go. And to stay away. "Jamie's back and settling in. He likes working for Dad. You don't need to worry."

Her mother shook her head. "That's my job, Vanessa. Some-day, when you have kids of your own, you'll understand that."

Understand, maybe. But she was never going to do this to her own children. She managed a tight smile.

"Vanessa. Good. We're all here now. Did you want some-thing to drink?" Her father sat, looking like a king on his throne.

"I'm fine. This isn't a six hour meeting, right?"

Jamie laughed. "Let's hope not."

"What a question, Vanessa." Her mother shook her head and

settled in the chair next to her father's. "Why don't you just start, James."

Her dad reached out and took her mother's hand. Vanessa's smile this time was genuine. For all their faults, she had to believe her parents loved each other. Maybe not in a way she understood, but it was there just the same.

He cleared his throat. "Vanessa, I've changed your trust back to the original age-only requirements."

Vanessa's eyebrows shot up. "Why? I mean, thank you. It'll be nice to have the money—although I don't need it. But what changed your mind?"

"Your brother has been on my case a little about it." Her dad turned and grinned at Jamie. "In a polite way, of course, but he's made it clear he considers it unjust. Particularly since he was the reason behind a new requirement for you, not your own behavior."

"Thanks, Jamie." Of course, she'd asked him not to worry about it—about her—but maybe big brothers weren't able to stop that kind of behavior.

"Also—" Vanessa looked back at her dad. There was more? "Given your relationship with Topher, and the fact that he had no issue signing a prenup, it seemed like you were on track to meet the new terms. Maybe not by your birthday, but it's not as if you're just floating around with no thought for your future."

"I—he—what?" Vanessa jolted to her feet and glared at her father. "I'm not sure where to begin responding to that."

"Oh, Vanessa, calm down." Her mother frowned. "None of this should be a surprise."

And yet, all of it was. "Do you realize the only reason I even have a relationship with Topher is because he agreed to pretend to date me to get you off my back for a little while?"

Her father leaned back, whether from shock or from the fact that Vanessa was leaning forward into his space, she wasn't sure.

"Nessa . . ."

She whirled and pointed a finger at her brother. "No. You stay out of this. You've done plenty already."

Jamie held up his hands and leaned back, crossing his legs.

"Did you know about this, Mom? The prenup thing?"

"Of course, honey. You didn't think we'd let you or your brother marry without protections in place, did you?"

"Let us? What makes you think you have any say in the matter? I'm not sixteen. I'm twenty nine. As much as I'd like to know you approved of anyone I married, it's not your choice or your decision." Vanessa crossed her arms and blinked away the spots dancing in front of her eyes. "And if you think any money you have makes a difference to me, you don't know me at all. My business—my little flower shop as you love to call it—does well. I'm supporting myself and making a profit, and considering hiring some help. Because I can afford to all on my own. So you know what? Keep your money and your prenup. I don't want either of them."

Vanessa strode from the room, her pace turning into a run as voices called out after her. She sprinted down the front steps to her car and slid behind the wheel.

Jamie ran up and knocked on the window.

She could just go. He'd move out of the way. Probably. She sighed and rolled down the window. "What?"

"Nessa."

She raised her eyebrows and waited.

Jamie closed his eyes then leaned forward and rested his forehead on the top of the car. He opened his eyes and met her gaze. "You know they love you."

"I know they think they do. But they have a lousy way of showing it."

"I won't argue with that. Come back inside."

"Would you? If they'd gone around your back to get your

girlfriend to sign a prenup before you'd even told her you loved her, would you go back inside?"

"You haven't told Topher you love him?"

"That's what you take away from that question?"

"Vanessa, come on. The guy's clearly crazy about you—why wouldn't you reciprocate?"

She sighed. If she couldn't explain it to herself, how was she supposed to explain it to her brother? "Because I don't know."

"What's to know? You like spending time with him, you're attracted, he shares the same beliefs as you, and you're in related industries so there will probably always be plenty to talk about. The more I look at couples who last—people like Mom and Dad —the more I'm convinced that successful marriages are as much a matter of determination as anything else. If you want to love him, if you choose that, then you just keep choosing it day after day."

"Says the guy with no romantic prospects on the horizon. Let it go, Jamie. This isn't your business. It's not Mom and Dad's business. It's mine and Topher's. Period." She revved the engine and shifted out of park.

Jamie stepped back, his shoulders drooping. "You're just going to go? What about the rest of the family meeting?"

"Seems to me Dad can handle it without me. That certainly seems to be his MO for everything else in my life."

24

Topher frowned and hit pause on his controller before reaching for the phone. Why anyone would be calling now was beyond him. Everyone had been busy when he tried to find someone to hang with while Vanessa went to her parents'. He probably could've tagged along. The thought crossed his mind once or twice, but since she didn't offer, he hadn't wanted to push. Besides, he wasn't family.

Yet.

He didn't recognize the number but swiped to answer the call anyway. The video game wasn't exactly holding his attention. "Hello?"

"Topher? It's Jamie, Vanessa's brother."

"Hey. I thought there was a family meeting?"

Jamie's laugh held no mirth. "There was. It's over. You're probably going to get an irate call. Dad brought up the prenup."

Topher winced. "Why would he do that?"

"I kind of understand what he was thinking, but it's like he forgot who Vanessa is for a minute."

"She's going to dump me, isn't she?" Topher's stomach twisted into knots. How had he miscalculated so badly? Step one, he hadn't counted on her dad bringing it up. "That wasn't the whole point of the meeting, was it?"

"No. Dad's officially retiring and I'm taking over his role completely. He wanted to explain everything to Mom and Vanessa together. I tried to convince him that Nessa didn't care, but Dad has to do things his way. He wanted everyone in the family to know ahead of the press release next Monday."

"Congratulations."

"Thanks, man. I'm looking forward to it. As for Vanessa, just be honest with her."

"I always have been." His phone beeped, signaling another call. "This might be her."

Jamie snorted. "Good luck."

Topher shot up a quick prayer and switched over. "Hey, Vanessa."

"Don't 'hey' me. How could you?"

"How could I what?" There was no point in letting her know Jamie had given him a head's up. It wasn't as if that gave him any particular insight. It was simply extra time for him to come up with worst-case scenarios.

"Jamie didn't call you? I know Jamie called you."

Topher sighed. "He did. I'm not sure why you're so upset."

"Seriously? Because you basically told my dad you were going to marry me and then signed a prenup. You and I have had a few conversations about marriage, but we haven't even looked at rings or talked about things like where we'd live. We're not at the fly to Vegas and get married stage of our relationship."

"I don't really want to get married in Vegas. We don't have to have a huge wedding, but I would like it to be in a church. Or I guess at Peacock Hill, if you wanted something outside."

"Do you think this is a joke? My dad thinks we're getting married, Topher. That's not funny."

The sick dread that had been swimming in his stomach

started to solidify into something closer to irritation. "If marrying me is so repugnant, I have to ask why we're dating. Is that why you won't tell me you love me? Because I'm in love with you, Vanessa. I want to make a life with you. So no, I didn't have a problem signing a stupid piece of paper that gives your father peace of mind, because I didn't see a point in time where it would even be relevant. I haven't been playing games with you. I didn't realize you were."

Vanessa sputtered. "Don't try and turn this around on me."

Topher bit back the words that wanted to spew out. He wasn't trying to turn it around. As far as he was concerned, it was on her.

"Say something."

"What do you want me to say, Vanessa? I love you. I thought you were struggling with the words, with being sure you meant them when you said them. I didn't realize you weren't even close to feeling them."

"No. That's not fair."

"You're right. It isn't. To either of us."

"Topher . . ."

So it wouldn't be her breaking up with him after all. "The prenup only matters if we get married. Right now it's just my signature on a hypothetical. Easy enough to shred. Maybe we need to step back and reevaluate."

"What are you saying?"

His eyes burned. He blinked and stared at his hands before balling them into fists. "I can still meet you at the ball on Saturday. I imagine finding another taker for the ticket this late would be a challenge. Figure out what you want and be ready to let me know, because we're both old enough that we don't need to waste our time on a relationship that's going nowhere. Between now and then, I think it'd be better for there to be no contact."

"But church tomorrow?"

"I'll go tonight." Topher pulled the phone from his ear and checked the time. He could still make it if he hurried. "You'll have to drive yourself, obviously."

"This isn't what I wanted to happen."

"What did you want?"

"I don't know."

"Figure it out by Saturday, Vanessa. For both our sakes." He ended the call and dropped his phone on the couch. He stared at the spaceship paused mid-battle on the TV and shook his head before clicking it off. He'd said he'd hit the Saturday evening service, so he'd go. Even if going to church was the absolute last thing he wanted to do.

That was usually when he needed it most.

"Trick or treat!" The kids on the stoop hollered in unison.

Topher smiled in spite of himself and dipped his hand into the bowl of candy he'd bought just for this purpose. Princesses and super heroes seemed to be the primary order of the evening, and this group was no different. Adults hovered in the background, reminding the kids to say thank you as they left.

"Topher, hang on a sec." Sean jogged around the edge of the cluster of kids and parents. "Figured you'd be here."

"Don't you get kids at your apartment?" Topher leaned against the door jamb. It'd be nice if Sean could hang out, but who wanted their door egged?

"I put out a big bowl and said to take two. Usually that works well enough."

"Where's Larissa?"

"Answering her own door. We weren't going to end up spending the evening together anyway, so we decided I should come see how you were. You've been scarce this week."

Topher studied his friend and pushed the door open a little wider. "Come on in. You talked to Vanessa on Sunday?"

"Larissa did. They ended up going to lunch together. I got filled in a little. Kept waiting for you to get in touch."

"Why, man? What are you going to do?" Topher opened the door to fill another round of pillowcases and plastic pumpkins.

"I don't know, be a friend." Sean shrugged. "Got any soda?"

"Yeah, bottom drawer of the fridge. No diet though."

Sean laughed. "Is that your way of suggesting I'm being a girl?"

"If the shoe fits." Topher grinned. "I'm not braiding your hair, either."

"Yeah, yeah." Sean grabbed a can and popped the top. "So. How's the ultimatum working for you?"

Topher scrubbed a hand over his face. He hadn't intended to give her an ultimatum, but that didn't change what happened. "About as well as they usually do, I guess. I mean, we're not talking until Saturday, so I don't even know."

"Ever consider giving her a call?"

Just about every second of every day. "Yeah, but what would it change? She needs to figure out why we're together. If we aren't on the same page, what's the point? I don't need to date someone just to say I'm not single. I want to be married. Have a family. If she doesn't?"

Sean nodded. "A prenup, huh?"

"I don't honestly see the big deal. If we get married, I'm not going to leave her. I believe marriage is forever. You work through the problems, even when they're hard. So what's the big deal about a paper that will never matter? Beyond that? I don't mind her having money. I don't want her money. If we got married, I'd hope she'd talk to me about how she wanted to spend it—but she wouldn't have to. It's hers. I don't have a problem with that." Topher fought the urge to sigh and went back to the door. He smiled at the kids as he handed out more candy.

"Did you tell her that?"

"I thought I had, yeah. I know I told her I love her."

"And?"

"And she smiled and patted my knee."

Sean winced.

"Exactly. I don't know what's happening on Saturday other than I'm putting on my tux and heading down to Peacock Hill. I always enjoy seeing the gang there and I imagine the house will be even fancier than it is for weddings, so that'll make the trip worthwhile."

"And Vanessa?"

"I guess I'll find out what she has to say when I get there." He didn't love that, but he'd given her the week and he was going to respect that. He needed her to be sure, whatever decision she made. "I've been praying we both have clear insight into God's will for our relationship. That's the only thing I know to do."

"That's the best thing you can do."

Topher opened another bag of snack size candy bars and dumped them into the bowl by the door. Time to change the subject and try to shift his mind away from Vanessa. "You figure out when you're going to propose yet?"

"I think tomorrow. I made reservations at that new little French place downtown. Simple, classic. Dinner and then just before dessert, I'll bring out the ring and ask." Sean pressed a hand to his belly. "I know she's going to say yes. There's no way she won't. But I'm still nervous."

Topher chuckled. "I think that just proves you're human."

"What are you going to do with the ring you bought?"

He'd been asking himself that question all week. He could take it back. Return it. It'd probably still be there if Vanessa decided to continue their relationship with the goal of marriage.

But he wanted it on her finger. He wanted to know they were on their way to making promises. "It might be stupid—it probably is—but I'm taking it with me on Saturday."

"To the ball."

Topher nodded.

"Why?"

"Because if Vanessa has decided she loves me, I want to give it to her."

"You don't think that's a little too fast? You basically broke up with her on Sunday."

"We didn't break up. We stepped back, so she could think and figure out what she wants. What I want hasn't changed. I don't know how else to prove that to her."

Sean shook his head. "Gutsy."

"Maybe. I guess we'll find out."

25

Vanessa took one final tour of the house. The peacock tail standing urns had turned out better than she'd imagined. Having real peacock feathers fanning through the flowers was the final little detail they'd originally been missing. A week with no distractions—no Topher—had given her a lot of time to think and design. And pray.

There'd been a lot of prayer.

Her mother had called a lot, too. As had her father.

By Wednesday she'd been willing to answer the phone and at least hear what they had to say. She still didn't love what they'd done—Topher included—but she understood it. A little.

The reality was she missed him. She'd picked up the phone to call him more times than she cared to count. And she'd driven past the bakery an embarrassing number of times.

If he wanted her to be sure, she was. She loved him. She wanted a future with him, and she didn't want to waste a lot of time waiting to get started.

Now she just had to hope he was still willing to give her another chance.

"Everything looks amazing." Claire came down the steps of

the grand staircase and brushed her fingers over a feather. "I knew you were good, but you've outdone yourself."

"Thanks. I'm really pleased. Is there a photographer coming?"

Claire nodded.

"Do you think you could ask them to take a few shots of the flowers during the event? I'd like something with people in the background so they're not as sterile as the ones I took." It would make better marketing. At least it seemed like it to her. She'd love to ask Topher what he thought—she'd taken the idea from his website. He had the more traditional close-ups of his cakes and desserts, but he also had more candid shots of people enjoying them. It added a friendlier touch to the album.

"Sure thing." Claire paused and furrowed her brow. "You okay?"

"Just tired." Vanessa was beyond tired. Physically that summed it up, but emotionally, she was wrung out. The past week had been entirely too much emotional upheaval. Now, at the end, she was ready for the resolution. Whatever that ended up being. "I'll be fine after tonight."

One way or another.

"Okay. Well, if I see you dateless, I'm going to come hang out with you. Apparently Danny's bringing Casey. Because I needed to have his girlfriend pushed in my face, I guess." Claire sighed. "Why can't I get over him? It's not like we ever dated."

Vanessa patted Claire's arm. "I'm sorry. I'll keep an eye out."

Claire's phone chimed and she glanced at it. "Gotta run. See you when things get swinging."

Vanessa took one last look in the dining room where Topher's magnificent cake held court on a table against the wall. Apparently he'd been down yesterday to deliver it with instructions for the caterers on assembly. It didn't look like they'd messed it up.

She headed around the stairs and out the door that led to the covered drop off area. It had a fancy French name she could never wrap her tongue around. Her mom would know. It wasn't portico. *Porte cochere*? Something along those lines. She double-checked the arrangements leading down the stairs to the gravel driveway that was now covered with round tables. Each table had a smaller version of the standing urns in the center, a tall peacock-blue taper spearing up out of the middle. It was a nice effect for people who wanted to sit and eat instead of wandering and mingling.

She climbed the stone steps that led up past the marble fountain to the raised gardens. She hadn't done as much here. There were concrete urns that she'd filled with flowers that could handle the cooler evening—although the weathermen were anticipating temperatures between sixty-five and seventy degrees until midnight. It wasn't as if they needed to be frost resistant.

A dance floor had been set up in front of the pergola that ran the width of the large space. If they kept to the usual pattern, there'd be a string quartet coming any minute now to provide appropriate waltzes, fox trots, and other old timey dance music. She'd lobbied, once, for the inclusion of more modern music. Maybe a DJ instead. Her mother had nearly lost her standing and had stepped down from the steering committee after that. Oops.

The Founder's Ball was traditional. And that was that.

Still, dancing under the stars was new. The venues before had always been completely indoors. Making it possible for, let alone encouraging, guests to spill outdoors was enough progress for one year.

"Has anyone told you it looks great?" Anna paused and looked out past the urns to the English garden beyond. "And the gardens are holding up. I was worried we'd be down to bare branches on everything."

Vanessa smiled. "I think it's going to be a big success."

"Hope so. Something like this has real potential for Peacock Hill. Claire has done so much to put us on the map. It's exciting to see where God's going to take things next."

"And your landscaping business?"

"Growing. Duncan's talking about hiring a full-time crew in the spring. I guess we'll see. I'm not convinced it's the right time. We don't have to decide today, though, so that's good."

"I should go and get dressed. I don't want Topher to get here before I'm ready."

"You and Topher? That's great. How's it going?"

"I guess we'll find out tonight."

VANESSA ACCEPTED a glass of punch from a circling server. It was fizzy and pink, a lot like the drink she'd been served throughout high school. Except there was no sherbet floating in hers. Maybe there was some in the punch bowl, wherever that was. There were also glasses of wine and champagne circling, but Claire had insisted there be some sort of non-alcoholic option. What would the organizers think of the addition?

The canapés were circling as well and guests were arriving in pairs and quartets. Where was Topher? He'd come, wouldn't he? He'd said he'd see her here. Maybe during the week he changed his mind . . . but wouldn't he have told her?

"So far, so good." Claire eased up to Vanessa's elbow and watched the front door with her. "At this point, it's completely out of my hands. But I saw one of the ladies from the steering committee slip one of your cards into her clutch. I'm going to consider it a seal of approval."

It could just as easily be a way for her to ensure she knew who to blame, but there was no point in saying that. Claire was nervous enough as it was. "It's going to be a raging success, I can already tell."

"Yeah, how?" Claire's chuckle trailed off. "Well, well. He cleans up nice."

Vanessa followed her gaze and the knot in her chest loosened. Topher did, in fact, clean up well. Everything about him was a sight for sore eyes—the tux was a bonus.

"Mmmhmm, and now he's seen you. I could be invisible. Look at him, so focused on you, the place could be empty. Here he comes. I guess that's my cue. Have fun tonight, Vanessa."

Vanessa tore her gaze away from Topher for a moment to smile at Claire before she faded into the crowd.

Topher wound his way through the crowd and stopped an arm's length away. "Hi. You look amazing."

Vanessa glanced down at the curve-skimming column dress in navy blue she'd found at the consignment store. She hadn't meant to stop there, but the dress had been in the window, and the off-the-shoulder neckline had caught her eye. She hadn't expected it to be her size. When it was, she'd had to try it on. Seeing the appreciation in Topher's eyes more than made up for the concern she'd had about a pre-owned dress. "Thanks. You too. I was starting to worry you wouldn't come."

"I told you I'd be here." Topher offered his hand. "Shall we?"

Vanessa slipped her hand into his. Warmth washed through her. She'd missed this. She squeezed his fingers as they wove through the growing crowd. "Want to go outside? There's a string quartet."

Topher's gaze fixed on something over her head and she started to turn. "No, don't look. Outside sounds like a good plan."

"What was that?" Vanessa gathered up the front of her dress

as she jogged to try and keep up with Topher's lengthening stride. "Topher, slow down. I'm wearing heels."

"Sorry." He slowed and ducked into a doorway built into the base of the stairs, tugging her close. His breath flowed past her ear. "Your parents. I didn't want to run into them just yet."

She bit her lower lip and fought the myriad of sensations. She swallowed. She should say hello to her parents. She'd forgiven them. Mostly. She was working on it, at least. But later would work, too. "Okay. They won't go outside. Mom doesn't believe an event like this should be outdoors."

Topher arched a brow but tugged her hand. "Then by all means, let's head out. The flowers are incredible. I imagine you'll be getting lots of new business from this."

She hoped so. It would be nice to recover some of the cost through future business. Cutting her prices to give Claire an edge was probably something she would've done even if she hadn't been able to put cards out here and there, but the little bit of advertising wasn't going to hurt. "Thanks. I guess we'll see. Did you consider bidding on the catering?"

He shook his head and steered them toward the stairs leading up to the garden. "I looked at it, but they want one vendor doing the food and desserts. I could hire a sub—I've done that occasionally for weddings where it was more cost effective—but it's not my preference. They let me put some cards by the cake, so it's not as if there's not a possibility of more business from that. Anyway, tonight I'm glad I get to spend time with you, not hang out in the kitchen supervising trays."

Vanessa eyed the dance floor where couples were already spinning in one another's arms. She could fake a few of the moves—her mother had insisted on cotillion classes—but would Topher even want to? Her gaze landed on the pergola. "Come on, let's go back here."

There were chairs set out under the twisting vines that

draped down from above and wound around the columns that supported the structure. Topher guided them to a corner and they sat, hands still linked.

Strains of a classical piece she probably ought to know drifted on the evening air. She looked over at Topher and met his gaze as he studied her.

"I'm sorry about Saturday."

He nodded once but didn't speak.

Vanessa pressed her lips together. This was harder than it should be. He wasn't making it any easier. Maybe he didn't want to. Her stomach dipped at the thought. There was only one way to find out. She cleared her throat. "I love you. I'm—please don't say you've changed your mind about me."

"I haven't. I'm not sure I could. I was really hoping you weren't going to put me in a position where I had to try." Topher scooted closer so their knees bumped. "At the risk of being pushy, I want to be sure I understand you. What about us?"

Vanessa's lips twitched. "I want a future together. You and me. The money—well, I stand by what I said to my dad when I told him he could keep it. He might, you know, just to teach me a lesson."

"I don't care about the money, Vanessa. Just you."

Vanessa took the first easy breath she'd had in a week. "Okay. We're okay."

"Almost. I have one more question."

She frowned. Another question meant another chance for her to mess things up again. She really didn't want that. She wanted him to kiss her and tell her it was okay. That they were going to be fine. They'd made it over a hurdle, why couldn't they celebrate it? "All right."

Topher slipped his hand into his pocket and pulled something free. He took both her hands and flipped them over, forming a cradle into which he placed a small velvet box.

Vanessa's breath caught and she flicked her gaze from the box to his eyes. Her heart hammered against her ribs. "Yes."

He chuckled. "You don't know what I'm going to ask yet."

Her eyes filled and a laugh bubbled out. "Sorry. I'll wait."

"I love you, Vanessa. Make a life with me. Make a family with me. Marry me." He flipped open the box and wiggled the ring free.

"Are you going to get to the question sometime soon?"

"Maybe it's more of a statement." Topher took her left hand and slid the ring down her finger. "But you already said yes, so I'm going to assume you're in agreement with it."

She held her hand up so the diamonds could sparkle in the low light and grinned. She put her hands on his cheeks and drew him close. "I love you, Topher. I'll make a life and a family with you. I can't think of anything I'd rather do."

Vanessa caught the flash of his grin before his lips caught hers and music swelled around them. Maybe it was the string quartet. Maybe it wasn't.

She didn't really care either way.

SNEAK PEEK OF A HEART RECONSIDERED

"That was some party."

Claire McIntyre turned, her mug of coffee steaming in the cool morning air. Of course it was Danny. He wore the shirt and pants from the tuxedo he'd worn to the Founder's Ball the night before, but the collar was open and the shirt untucked. His feet were bare. None of that should have a little curl of interest blooming in her belly. But it did.

She gave herself a mental shake and pushed a polite smile onto her lips. "I can't take the credit. We just provided the venue."

His eyebrows lifted. "And organized the details. I've seen you running around the last six weeks.

Claire took a sip from her mug and watched the mist around the base of the lion head fountain that spanned the back of Peacock Hill. He'd been watching her? When? "Yeah, well, that's what I do. I handle details."

"You're good at it." Danny tucked his hands in his pockets and turned to lean against the stone rail on the edge of the portico.

"Thanks." Now that he was facing her instead of standing

beside her, Claire couldn't avoid making eye contact. She glanced down. "Aren't your feet freezing? You should go inside before you catch cold."

Danny laughed. "Okay, Mom." He pushed off the rail and took a step toward the door. "Who was that guy you were dancing with last night?"

She'd danced with a lot of different men at the ball. Once word got out she'd been the organizer on the venue side, she hadn't had much time to sit and rest her feet. Apparently, thank you dances were a thing. But she'd only danced with one person more than once—the one man who was there without a date. "Jamie Fisher. Vanessa's brother."

"Vanessa the florist?"

Claire nodded.

"Huh. Okay." He paused, hand on the doorknob and waited until she met his gaze to speak. "It really was a nice event."

"I'm glad you and Casey had a good time. Did she stay the night, too?" She hadn't meant to ask that. Claire took another sip of coffee and tried to act casual.

"Not like you mean. You really think I'd do that? Here of all places?" Danny shook his head. "She stayed out in the tower. I was here. Upstairs on the third floor. Wow."

Heat washed over her face, but she refused to back down. "How would I know?"

"I thought you knew me. Guess I was wrong." He disappeared back inside.

Claire sighed, her shoulders sagging. "Yeah, well, so was I."

AT THE TAP on her office door Monday morning, Claire minimized the window on her computer screen. "Come in."

Deidre poked her head in and grinned. "That was some shindig Saturday night."

Claire laughed. "Swanky, right? But I've already had an email from the board chair and co-chair. They both let me know they'll be recommending us to the committee as a permanent venue."

"Really?" Deidre's eyes lit up and she stepped completely in the room. She high-fived Claire before settling in one of the chairs facing Claire's desk. "That's excellent. Is it always November? It's a good time for us—weddings are down and there aren't as many groups looking to stay."

"Yep. First Saturday of November. It's not a done deal, but their recommendation is going to help. A lot." Claire studied her sister. The woman was an inspiration. She'd put it all on the line several times—first when she took over their dad's handyman business and turned it into a regional success that had reality TV calling. And then, when the host of that show ended up elbowing her out and trying to steal all the profit, she'd sold and come down to Peacock Hill to start over. Only Deidre could have seen the ramshackle shell of a building and imagined what it could look like with a little—or a lot—of elbow grease. And then she'd made it happen. "I'm proud of you, you know that?"

Dee flushed a pretty pink. "Yeah, well, same goes. As far as I'm concerned, you do all the hard work."

"Nuh-uh. You know me. I can grout tile, but that's about where my handyness ends. You made Peacock Hill what it is. It's an amazing accomplishment."

"Well, you took it and ran with it. A gorgeous mansion doesn't do a whole lot of good if it can't support you. I might have restored the place, but you brought it back to life." Deidre cocked her head to the side. "What's going on?"

"What do you mean?"

"I mean you can be complimentary, but you don't usually

push it. If I didn't know better, I'd say you were buttering me up before leaving."

Claire froze.

"Now is when you laugh." Deidre paled. "Laugh, Claire, before it's not funny."

"Here's the thing."

"No." Deidre lurched to her feet, her pregnant belly making the action less graceful than she would normally have been. "There's no thing. Things are not allowed. I can't do this without you. I don't *want* to do this without you. So don't you even think about saying you're going to leave me."

Claire watched tears drip down her sister's face and her shoulders sagged. She'd known this would happen. It was hormones. Pregnancy hormones were something she was becoming intimately familiar with during her sister's pregnancy. That didn't mean she was immune to the guilt they spurred. "But Dee . . ."

"Don't." Deidre held up one hand while she used the other to wipe her face. "I can't talk about this right now. I can't believe you'd even think about doing this to me. To us!"

Her mouth opened and she drew in a breath to speak, letting it back out slowly when her sister stormed from the room and slammed the door home like a shot. "That went well."

Claire drummed her fingers on her desk before reopening her resume on her computer. There was no harm in having a resume. It didn't mean she was definitely going to leave. It provided options. Options were good things, weren't they?

She spent thirty minutes fiddling with the document before she pushed away from the desk with a groan. This was just one of the problems with family businesses. She'd never needed a resume before. Now, here she was in her late twenties with no clue how to make one people would put on the top of a pile. Oh, sure, the internet was full of ideas and recommendations, but how was she supposed to know which ones were the right ones?

Vanessa.

The answer was so obvious! Claire grabbed her phone and considered. A text was her preference, but how long would it take Vanessa to get back to her? As far as Claire knew, her friend was planning to open her flower shop as usual. So. A call. She tapped the phone icon and waited as it rang.

"Hey, Claire."

"Hey. Do you have a second?"

"Sure. It's quiet this morning. What's up?"

"You come from a business-oriented family, right? Do you know anything about resumes?"

"A little, I guess. Why?"

"Because I'm working on one and I don't know if it's any good. Or what I'm missing. Or anything like that. There are people I could hire and get help, but I don't want to make that investment unless I have to."

"Send it to me and I'll look. Or—hey—I could pass it to my brother. He's the business king. He'd be able to give you better feedback than me."

Claire pressed her lips together. Jamie. She got a little quiver in her belly. She'd gone over her dances with him on Saturday night more than once when she'd had some free time—and when she was supposed to be focused on something else—since then. "Yeah. Sure. That'd be good. Thanks."

"No problem. Want me to just give you his email? Cut out the middle man?"

Did she? "You don't want to see it?"

"Honestly? You're better off with Jamie."

"All right." Claire opened the desk's middle drawer and retrieved a pad of sticky notes and a pen. "Go ahead."

Vanessa rattled off the email and Claire jotted it down. "Got it?"

Claire read it back.

"That's it. And there's someone at the door—let me know how it goes."

With a chuckle, Claire ended the call. She stared at the email address for the space of several heartbeats before taking a deep breath and opening a new email message on the computer.

She'd send it off and get back to work. There was a group of five writers coming on Thursday for a four-day retreat and she still had a few final details to see to before then.

If some small part of her hoped Jamie would use the phone number at the top of her resume to reach out personally, well, that couldn't be helped. The guy was gorgeous. And kind. And smart.

And not Danny.

That last one was important. Moving on from Danny was the top item on her to-do list for the end of the year.

WANT A FREE BOOK?

If you'd like to read another of my books, I'd love to have you join my newsletter. As a thank you for signing up, you'll receive a special short story that's unavailable anywhere else as well as a copy of one of my other books.

You can join via the form on my website.

ACKNOWLEDGMENTS

It's funny, before I ever published a book, I used to make a point of reading author acknowledgments. I loved seeing who got thanked and all the little tidbits authors sometimes put into this page.

Now that I have to write them, I find I do less reading of them. I think it's because I realize how woefully inadequate they are. I can never possibly thank everyone who was a part of making this book a reality — but let's give it a go.

First and always, I'm so thankful to my husband and kids. They give me space to write, they let me talk through ideas when I'm stumped (even though not a single one of them actually care a whit about romance), and they're generally unconcerned if we end up with Mac and cheese for dinner more often than is probably healthy.

Thanks also to the best friend/beta reader/critique partner I could ever imagine, Valerie Comer. Additional huge thanks to Heather Gray, Jan Elder, and Lynnette Bonner for their help in making this book make sense and keeping me from doing things like having Topher bake a cake in probably 5 minutes. (Don't we all wish?) If there's something in here that is ridiculous, it's absolutely not their fault.

Thanks are also owed to my mom. She's been gone about a year now, but it was her encouragement that spurred me on to take these books I write and make them available to the broader world. I have always and will always write for my own pleasure. I don't know if I ever would have written for yours without her influence. Miss you, mama.

Finally, and really this should probably have been first, thanks to Jesus for continuing to give me words to put down on the page. It's my prayer that something in here will encourage someone out there to walk a little closer to You.

ABOUT THE AUTHOR

Elizabeth Maddrey is a semi-reformed computer geek and homeschooling mother of two who lives in the suburbs of Washington D.C. When she isn't writing, Elizabeth is a voracious consumer of books. She loves to write about Christians who struggle through their lives, dealing with sin and receiving God's grace on their way to their own romantic happily ever after.

ALSO BY ELIZABETH MADDREY

Hope Ranch Series

Hope for Christmas

Peacock Hill Romance Series

A Heart Restored

A Heart Reclaimed

A Heart Realigned

A Heart Redirected

Arcadia Valley Romance – Baxter Family Bakery Series

Loaves & Wishes

Muffins & Moonbeams

Cookies & Candlelight

Donuts & Daydreams

The 'Operation Romance' Series

Operation Mistletoe

Operation Valentine

Operation Fireworks

Operation Back-to-School

The 'Taste of Romance' Series

A Splash of Substance

A Pinch of Promise

A Dash of Daring

A Handful of Hope

A Tidbit of Trust

The 'Grant Us Grace' Series

Joint Venture

Wisdom to Know

Courage to Change

Serenity to Accept

Pathway to Peace

The 'Remnants' Series:

Faith Departed

Hope Deferred

Love Defined

Stand alone novellas

Kinsale Kisses: An Irish Romance

Luna Rosa (part of A Tuscan Legacy)

For the most recent listing of all my books, please visit my website.